Frankie, Peaches and Me

Stella Etc.

Karen McCombie

Frankie, Peaches and Me

Stella Etc.

SCHOLASTIC

For Kirsty Etc.
(Amanda + Tim)

Scholastic Children's Books
An imprint of Scholastic Ltd
Euston House, 24 Eversholt Street
London, NW1 1DB, UK
Registered office: Westfield Road, Southam, Warwickshire, CV47 0RA
SCHOLASTIC and associated logos are trademarks and/or registered
trademarks of Scholastic Inc.

First published in the UK by Scholastic Ltd, 2004
This edition published in the UK by Scholastic Ltd, 2010

Text copyright © Karen McCombie, 2004
The right of Karen McCombie to be identified as the author of this work
has been asserted by her.

ISBN 9781407117768

A CIP catalogue record for this book is available from the British Library.
All rights reserved.

Printed in the UK by CPI Bookmarque, Croydon, Surrey.
Papers used by Scholastic Children's Books are made from wood grown in
sustainable forests.

3 5 7 9 10 8 6 4 2

This is a work of fiction. Names, characters, places, incidents and dialogues are products of
the author's imagina   g or

Contents

From: *stella*
To: Frankie
Subject: Hellooooooooooo!
Attachments: "Frankie, Peaches & Me"

Hi Frankie!

Sorry I missed your call – we were all out for a walk down at the beach (got a ton of sand in my ears from play-fighting with Jake and Jamie – still can't hear properly).

So on the message you left you said you had a dream about me last night: you dreamt I'd never moved away from London? Well, I guess there are mornings when I wake up and listen to the sound of the sea and the gulls and think, "Er, where am I again?"

But you coming to visit right after we moved here, that was great. OK, so it wasn't great *all* the time, specially not when we were arguing. But when you're marooned 50 metres in the air for half an hour, I guess you've got to pass the time somehow! I know we talked a lot and made up and everything, but anyway, I thought I'd scribble stuff down (see attachment); just stuff about what exactly happened that first week –

you know, the move here, and about Peaches, and Sugar Bay and you and . . . and the rest.

Oops, got to go – I might have half a beach in my ear but I can *definitely* hear somebody somewhere screaming (wish Jamie would grow out of this annoying biting thing). E-mail me back soon, and in the meantime, give your mum a big cuddle from me, send hugs to Neisha and Lauren and everyone, and . . . well, maybe you could say "hi" to Seb next time you see him (if that's not too weird, I mean). . .

Miss you ☹, but m8s 4eva ☺!

stella

PS Peaches says no hard feelings. (He *actually* said "Prrrp!", but I'm pretty sure that's what he meant!)

Chapter 1

Just your non-normal, un-average Saturday morning...

"Tinkle, tinkle, lickle star...!" Jake crooned in my ear, wafting a toy dumper truck in time to his song, and occasionally thunking it against the side of my head.

My little brother (one of a matching set) was completely oblivious to what was going on, but *I* wasn't. It was Saturday, it was 11.05 a.m., and it was the start of my brand new life. Worse luck.

Meanwhile, in a galaxy far, far away (OK, North London), my friends were probably doing the usual Saturday morning stuff.

Eleni would still be in bed, having a lie-in. (Though how she can sleep while her brother parps his weekend trumpet practice, I just don't know.)

Neisha would be in bed as well, but wide awake, watching telly and getting herself and her duvet covered in toast crumbs.

Lauren would be watching telly too, only in her living room, with her sister, fighting over the remote control (in a battle of boy bands v cartoons).

Parminder would be at the supermarket, helping her mum do the shopping, daydreaming about cute stuff in TopShop while cruising the frozen food aisle.

Frankie . . . well, round about this time in the morning, Frankie would be thinking about texting everyone to see who was up for a trek to the West End or a mooch around Camden Market in the afternoon. Of course, her Saturday morning would be a bit different just this once, 'cause she'd be clearing up from the party last night. My leaving party – and already it felt like for ever ago. . .

"So, Stella . . . what do you think?" Dad grinned at me hopefully, like a little kid who's showing you his model of the Tower of London made out of toilet-roll tubes.

I knew Dad wanted me to say something about the house (um, preferably something *nice* about the house), but all I could think of was what a deeply *non*-normal, *un*-average Saturday morning I was having. I mean, I'd got up at six in a practically empty-of-furniture house, watched some removal men cart away our beds to a waiting lorry, waved goodbye to the place I'd lived in and loved for the 13 years and two months I'd been on the planet, and sat for four hours in our car getting a numb bum and listening to a CD called *Really Annoying Nursery Rhymes That Will Drive You Insane* on a loop.

And now I was here, walking across the crunchy gravel of the driveway with a wriggly toddler in my arms, trying not to cry (I really don't think that was the reaction Dad – or Mum – would have wanted).

"Andy!" Mum shouted, as she lifted another wriggly toddler out of the car. "The removal lorry is here – but I think it's got stuck trying to get round the bend in the lane. Can you go and give the guys a hand?"

I don't know what Dad was meant to do – get a giant hacksaw and cut bits off the side of the lorry so it could get around the corner without scraping the ice-cream-coloured shades of paint off the terrace of tiny cottages next door to us, maybe? Or waft a magic potion at the lorry and make it shrink like something out of *Alice in Wonderland*?

Speaking of fairy tales, I felt like I'd found

myself stuck in the middle of one now, and I *don't* mean that in a good way. Apart from spying a sprawling council estate on the way into the town, the main part of Portbay – the place I was now supposed to think of as "home" – seemed like a higgledy-piggledy, claustrophobic jumble of tiny lanes and centuries-old cottages that tumbled downhill towards the sea. And here was *our* centuries-old cottage, like the house in *Hansel and Gretel*, minus the sweets, but looking suspiciously like a witch might be peeking out of one of the upstairs gabled windows at us.

"It's just perfect, isn't it?" Mum sighed, as she let Jamie slither his wriggling way out of her arms and on to the ground.

Perfect? Perfect for a *Houses from Hell* documentary on the telly. Or the set of a murder mystery, maybe.

"Mmm," I mumbled in reply, wondering if Mum had gone completely mad. The whole building was tatty and crumbly, and I kind of suspected it was only standing upright thanks to the creeping dark-green ivy that was clinging and clawing its way all over it.

"Maybe it's just as well you couldn't come that weekend when we first viewed the place – it's more

6

of a surprise for you now!" Mum smiled, reaching over and taking Jake out of my arms before he blinded me with the scoop of his dumper truck.

"Mmm," I mumbled again, glad that it was so sunny. It meant that I could shield my eyes as I pretended to survey the house, and hide the fact that tears were threatening again.

As far as your average parents went, Mum and Dad were great – they were groovier and trendier than any of my mates' mums and dads. They were interested in fashion and music and stuff, which my mates' parents definitely weren't. They were easy to talk to – when they weren't too busy with work or the boys, which was a *lot* of the time. But no matter how cool Mum and Dad were, when it came down to it, they were adults, and I was 13; there were two of them and just one of me, and so when they decided to move from London to Portbay, I really, *really* didn't have a choice. Course I told them I didn't want to go, and cried in front of them at the hideous idea of leaving Kentish Town and Frankie and all my other friends, but it didn't do any good. They just smiled, and hugged me and told me they understood – which translated as, "Sorry, but it's still going to happen, Stella!" After that, I just went quiet on the whole subject of the move, ignoring it as much as possible, pretending I had projects to finish and tests to study for and hiding out at Frankie's whenever Mum and Dad came down to Portbay to house-hunt.

"Are you going to call Frankie and let her know you got here OK?" Mum asked, noticing that I was fishing in the pocket of my denim skirt for my mobile.

"Mmm," I mumbled, forcing a lookalike smile on my face and turning away.

Frankie always teased me that my silver flip-topped phone looked like one of the phasers out of *Star Trek*. I wished it was – then instead of just talking to her, I could ask her to beam me back to London at the speed of light. Or quicker, if possible.

But my heart sank as Frankie's please-leave-a-message kicked in. And it sank even more with full-on, heart-squeezing, gut-wrenching home-sickness when I listened to it.

"Hi guys! I'm having way too much fun to answer the phone right now, so say what you've gotta say and I'll get back to you! Byeeeee!"

I wished I was back in London having fun with Frankie, instead of being marooned in this freaky little town. I wished I was at her flat now, helping her hoover up crisp crumbs instead of watching Mum rushing to stop Jamie from eating the gravel in our new driveway.

But at least I had one thing, I suddenly remembered, patting the cord bag on my shoulder, where I'd stashed the photo from last night.

The photo of that amazing moment when –

KEEERRRRRRRR-UNCH!

"Omigod!" Mum gasped, glancing around in the direction of the lane with dread.

Well, *that* was a good impression to make on our new neighbours – gouging a chunk out of their wall with our furniture lorry before we'd even moved in. Hey, I might *not* be the only person wishing my family had stayed in London. . .

Chapter 2

Oh, we don't like to be beside the seaside. . .

I was holding Jamie upside-down by the ankles – so that the make-up he'd nicked from my bag would fall out of his pockets – when I heard Mum say something on the phone downstairs.

Well, it was more a case of her saying nothing. And that told me *plenty*.

"Me next! Me next!" Jake suddenly demanded over the top of Jamie's giggles.

"Shh!" I tried to hush my brothers, ignoring the fact that Jake had what looked suspiciously like a pair of my knickers fastened to his head with a used section of parcel tape (he must have ripped it off one of the cardboard boxes). Honestly, trying to unpack with these two around was as easy as nailing jelly to a tree. And when it came to getting them to shut up, I had *no* chance.

"Well, the neighbours probably secretly hate us, but they acted very sweet when we offered to pay for the damage. Oh, our place? Well, it's messy and nothing works, and we're in total chaos, but it's fine."

(*That* was the chunk of Mum's conversation I'd tuned into when I first spotted Jamie shoving my mascara and strawberry lipgloss into his dungaree pockets.)

"Hey, you know what Andy's like, Vanessa – he can't *wait* to get started on the place. He's already eyeing up the sledgehammer, and the removal lorry's still in the driveway!"

(Auntie Vanessa hadn't wasted much time – we'd only left London six hours ago and here she was on the phone, pummelling Mum for an update on the Big Move.)

"The boys?"

(Auntie V must have been asking about Jake and Jamie.)

"They're having a great time – they've been thundering up and down the stairs, and getting in everyone's way!"

(And mostly wrecking what little of my room I'd managed to get halfway organized – which Mum and Dad thought was fine, since it distracted Jamie from biting the removal men and Jake from escaping our clutches and shouting "Boo!" at all the cars coming along the narrow lane next to the house.)

11

"Stella? Oh, you know what she's like – not saying much. . ."

And that's when I *really* started to pay attention – that moment when Mum tapered off and Auntie V must have been talking in her ear instead. I started listening to the silence so hard that I almost forgot that I was holding a wriggling, giggling small boy by the legs (two year olds are surprisingly heavy, by the way).

"Ah, Stella, my little star. . ." I bet Auntie V would've been saying. Or make that *sighing*. That's my Aunt Vanessa's catchphrase when it comes to me, just like she calls out, "Oh, no! Here come the Muppets!" whenever Jamie and Jake come charging anywhere near her. But the difference is, when she's calling Jake "Gonzo" and my more bite-happy brother "Animal", she's doing it with a big grin of affection on her face. When she smiles at me ruefully and sighs her "Ah, Stella, my little star. . ." sigh, I know she's saying it with a big dollop of irony. How come? Well, 'cause of my name, of course. Stella means "star", and the trouble is, I'm anything *but*. I mean, I know Auntie V's really *fond* of me and everything, but I always get the feeling that she's just a *tiny* bit disappointed with me, a bit like a lioness who's discovered that her cub is a broccoli-nibbling vegetarian. . .

So where did Mum and Dad get the inspiration for that name? Well, not from one star; from a few billion, to be precise. The night they took me home from hospital, while I was snoozing and dreaming newborn dreams, they gazed wistfully out of the window, and were amazed to see a sky full of twinkling, sparkling planets. I know the sky is *always* full of them, but when you live in a big city like London, most nights you're more likely to see just some swirly orange glow of the street-lights reflected in clouds than the Big Dipper. And so either Mum or Dad (they argue about which one it actually was) gawped skyward, got inspired, landed me with the name "Stella" and it stuck.

Auntie V loved it. I mean LOVED it. But then Auntie V is generally star-struck anyway. Dad told me that when they were growing up, Auntie V's one burning desire in life was to perform in West End musicals like *Les Miserables* and *Chicago* and stuff. He said she had all the drive and ambition (as well as the figure and looks) to do it. The only thing that held her back was the fact that – stunning and determined as she was – she had all the co-ordination of a walrus on dry land when it came to dancing and a singing voice like a duck with its head in a bucket. So she ditched her big plans and did the next best thing instead, becoming an *agent* for people who worked in musicals like *Les Miserables* and *Chicago* and stuff. And then when her first niece was born (me) and ended up with this particular name (Stella), Auntie V decided it was all fate, and that I would grow up and fulfil her every dream and ambition and be the star that she never was.

Er. . .

Unfortunately for Auntie V, I turned out to be the shyest person I know. I mean, *inside* my head, I'm this chatty person with plenty to say and smart, killer lines that would have everyone cracking up – if they could only hear them. At my old school, I always left the gags and the chatting to Frankie and Lauren and Neisha or whoever. They never minded me being the quiet one of our crowd. (Hey, maybe I was so quiet they wouldn't even notice I'd gone. . .?)

"The good thing is that it's the holidays, so she's got the whole summer to settle in," I heard Mum say. Peeking through the banisters I could see that she was now stepping over some boxes and picking her way into the living room. "Well, of *course* I know it's going to be hard for her, Vanessa. I *know* it's tough to be 13 and have to start over."

Hmm, sounded like Auntie V was sticking up for her shy little Stella the "star" . . . which wasn't a big surprise, considering. I mean, when Mum and Dad announced that they were selling up and moving us all to Portbore (sorry, Port*bay*), Auntie V had laughed out loud. "Yeah, *right*! Like you two would *really* give up your home, your careers, your friends, etc., just like that!" she'd grinned, thinking my parents were only fooling around with this talk of new starts and bracing sea air. She'd *stopped* laughing when they pulled out the estate agents' details for this half-derelict pile of bricks and woodworm that was supposed to be a "cottage of real character". And she went positively *white* after that, frowning so hard her forehead looked all corrugated, before choking out, "Is someone *paying* you to move into this cattle shed?"

It's fair to say that Auntie V prefers sarky to subtle. She always says what's on her mind – unlike me, who always thinks what I never say. So even though there were times when Auntie V could be so sarcastic it made me *wince*, I just loved the fact she came out with stuff to do with the move that *I* never would in a zillion years. Like wondering aloud why anyone sane would want to leave one of the biggest, most bustling cities in Europe for one of the most decrepit, dullsville old towns on the south coast.

("The kids will love growing up by the seaside!" Dad had argued. Um . . . you want a bet, Dad?)

She'd demanded to know why anyone would want to move away from tons of multiplex cinemas that showed everything from the newest Disney film to the biggest Bollywood epic, and settle in a town that probably didn't even have a *video* shop.

("The simpler life will be better for us." Speak for yourself, Dad.)

"And what about all the culture your kids are going to miss out on?" Auntie V had pointed out, reminding my parents that only last week in Camden, our family had got dirty looks in a Moroccan restaurant, 'cause Jamie and Jake had had a food fight with couscous. From now on, the most exotic place we'd be asked to leave would be the fish and chip shop on the seafront.

("We'll bond more as a family," Mum had tried to explain to Auntie V – who snorted as loudly as *I'd* have liked to.)

But all of Auntie V's sarcastic jokes about us swapping a cool, split-level flat in Kentish Town for a broken-down house round the corner from the back of beyond fell on totally deaf ears. So last week, I'd started to take down the posters from my lilac-painted walls, and now I was going to have to put those same posters back up on walls that didn't have any paint on them at all. Or *plaster*, for that matter.

And, worse than swapping walls for rubble, I'd been forced to swap the best bunch of friends a girl could have (that's *you*, Frankie, Lauren, Eleni, Neisha, Parminder) for . . . *no one*. No one at all. And even someone as upfront and confident as Auntie V would find that tough. But when you're *me*, it's just about the scariest thing *ever*. . .

"Kissy kissy boy!"

For a second, I didn't know what Jake was on about: what with Mum disappearing into the living room and out of earwigging range, I'd only just noticed that Jamie – happy as he was to be dangling upside-down – was now going a horrible shade of plum, thanks to all the blood rushing to his head.

I whirled my little brother the right way round, and got down on my knees, holding his shoulders in case he had an attack of the wobbles. But as soon as he grinned and said *"Again!"* I knew that he was all right.

17

And that's when I saw – out of the corner of my eye – what Jake was up to. . .

"Give that to me, Jake!" I ordered, feeling my blood run ice-cube cold as I spotted the photo he was clutching between his sticky fingers.

Stupid, stupid, *stupid*.

When either of my brothers gets hold of something they shouldn't, there's no way of negotiating with them. All you can do is ignore them till they get bored and dump whatever it is; bribe them; or use brute force (i.e. hold them upsidedown till their ill-gotten gains tumble out of their pockets).

"Stella kissy kissy boy!" Jake giggled, holding the photo away from me in one hand while pulling a trailing section of parcel tape away from the eyelid it had just stuck itself to.

"*I'll* do that for you, Jake," I offered, letting go of Jamie (who immediately fell over in a dizzy, sniggering pile), and reaching across to help disentangle the parcel tape from Jake's face.

Actually, it was more a case of "Boy kissy kissy Stella" – and only kissy kissy on the cheek – but that wasn't important right now. What *was* important was that this was my chance: I knew that if I pretended not to notice that Jake was holding on to the one, the *only* photo I had of Seb (it looked like Jake must have been raiding my bag alongside Jamie), then I *might* manage to snatch it back off him before he ate it or gave it to one of the removal men.

"Sticky," mumbled Jake, pointing to the tape holding my knickers on his head.

"I know, Jake," I muttered sympathetically, realizing that this was going to work. One swift flick of the tape, and he'd be so gruesomely fascinated by the fact that half his eyelashes were attached to the gluey brown tape that I'd be able to retrieve Seb, or all I had of him.

Hey, bad timing! Love S xxx he'd scrawled on the back of the Polaroid, taken at my leaving party last night.

Bad timing?! The understatement of the *century*, I think. . . I'd only been in love with Seb for a year, and he practically tells me he feels the same when I'm due to move out of London in a few hours' time!

"There . . . gently does it," I murmured softly, as I slowly loosened the tape with one hand and reached across for the photo with the other.

Then again. . .

Did you know that two and a bit year olds

have lightning reflexes? Before I got any further with Jake, I felt Jamie's fat little finger squish something on my chin and bottom lip – by the sweet smell of it, it was half of the pot of strawberry lipgloss he must have retrieved from the landing floor. I'd just tried to gently push his hand away before his finger reached my nostril when a jolt of pain shot up my arm.

"*Jamie!*" I heard Dad call loudly from the front doorway downstairs. "How many times do I have to tell you?! Biting is very, *very* bad!"

"Sowwy, Stewwa!" Jamie lisped appealingly at me, as he stroked my hair like I was a cat.

"RaaaaRRRGGGHHH!" Jake roared meantime, hurtling himself feet-first, face-to-the-floorboards down the stairs towards Dad and the TV set he was carrying into the house.

The knickers still taped to Jake's head flopped in time to him thumping his way at top speed down each step. And the Polaroid? Well, all I could see of it was a crumpled white edge peeking from Jake's tiny clenched fist.

"Bye, Seb. . ." I whispered in my mind, as the baby-toothed dent in my arm throbbed madly.

Bye, the whole of my old life.

And hello . . . *what* exactly?

Chapter 3

The pong, the party and the squished Polaroid

A message from Frankie – *yesss!*

Soz – gran visited, couldn't call back earlier, I read on the tiny screen of my mobile. *So what's new house like? F x.*

The predictive text doodah on my phone didn't know what to make of the reply I was typing in. But *Bleurghhhhhh!* was the only – made-up – word that fitted the way I felt about my "home" just now.

Why bleurghhhhh? Frankie texted back. *Tell me l8r – going out now and mobie needs charging. Talk 2moz!*

Seven o'clock on Saturday night, and Frankie was off out, meeting up with Neisha and everyone, while I was here, all alone in my room. My room which smelled of cardboard, damp, Dettol and kiddie sick (*bleurghhhhh!*) – not the sort of combination of whiffs that Christian Dior or some other fancy scent company would exactly be rushing to capture for their latest perfume.

The cardboard smell was 'cause of the cardboard boxes all my worldly possessions were crammed into (hadn't quite worked up the enthusiasm to empty them *all* yet). The damp was 'cause . . . well . . . we'd moved into a mildewed shack of a house ("But think of all the history in this place, Stella! All the charm!" Mum had cooed when I pointed out the historic, charming black mould on the bathroom wall). The Dettol smell was the aftermath of Jamie eating half a jar of raspberry jam and a small bar of soap and then choosing *my* room to vomit up the red, foamy mess after a tiring chase by my concerned mum and dad. Who at this point – after clearing up the gunk on my threadbare carpet and then the pizza boxes from our tea – had decided to go out for an evening stroll and explore the delights of Portbore.

My parents had been *well* chuffed when I offered to babysit, specially after Jamie's spectacular barfathon. But the way *I* saw it, the boys were safely asleep now (only violently erupting volcanoes could wake them once they zonked into their synchronized night-time comas). And anyway, from what I'd seen of it so far, exploring the delights of Portbore would only take about seven minutes.

But for the moment – apart from the pong – I

was quite enjoying those precious seven minutes of peace and not having to smile and pretend to my parents that I was OK-ish and not completely gutted about moving here.

Wonder whose house Frankie's going round to tonight? I thought miserably, as I struggled to open the welded-shut window in my room, desperate to get some clean, fresh air in the place. *Will they be talking about the party? Will they be talking about me and Seb. . .?*

"He's coming, y'know!" Frankie had grinned at me in class yesterday afternoon, on the last day of term, on my last day in London. (Sniff. . .)

"He is *not!*" I'd spluttered, trying to convince myself that Frankie was winding me up. But I knew that no matter *how* loud and lairy my best friend was, she wouldn't be so cruel as to tease me about Seb coming to my leaving party. Would she?

Course she wouldn't. And so later, at Frankie's house, surrounded by my gang of girls, a whole bunch of people from our year that Frankie had invited along, and surfaces *groaning* under the weight of the party food Frankie's mum had made for us, I just about fainted when I saw Seb walk in. He was smiling his usual, gorgeous, lopsided smile, but – wow – he was smiling at *me*. . .

"I can't believe he's here!" I'd whispered to Frankie, as I watched Seb amble off to the kitchen with his mate to get something to drink.

"Call it a leaving present from me!" Frankie had laughed.

She'd been chatting to him earlier on in the week, in the lunchtime scrum at the kebab shop on the High Street. Seb was cool that way – he might be in the year above us at school, but he wasn't the type of guy to look down on you like you were way down on the food chain just because you were younger. He always said stuff like, "Hi, how you doing?" to me and my mates. Pity I was too crippled with shyness and longing to say anything in reply apart from "Eee!" (loosely translates as a very, *very* shy "hi!"). Luckily, Frankie doesn't have that problem. Frankie can talk to anyone – parents, teachers, gorgeous boys like Seb – like they're all old friends of hers. And so on Tuesday, over a finger-scorchingly hot shish kebab, Frankie had invited Seb to the party she was holding for me.

And *boy*, would I be for ever grateful to Kismet Kebabs and my best friend for that. . .

"You know something?" Seb grinned at me in that adorable lopsided way of his, when he finally came over, later on in the night.

I didn't – i.e. didn't *dare* – say anything in reply, and hoped a smile would be enough to get him to carry on. It was, lucky for me.

"I always thought you were kind of cute, Stella."

Miraculously, I didn't fall in a crumpled pile at his feet, and even managed to mumble an awkward, "Oh. . ." It wasn't much, but I hoped Seb realized that it meant, "I think the same way about you!" Course it *might* have helped if I'd looked him in the eye and not the kneecaps when I said it. . .

And then Frankie – who'd made this mad, magical moment happen in the first place – managed to ruin it totally by pointing her dad's ancient Polaroid camera in our direction and blinding me and Seb with the flash. I was just trying to blink away the white, fuzzy-edged splodges swirling in front of my eyes when two things happened; first, I heard Seb's mate yell at him to hurry up 'cause he wanted to leave, and then – *wow, wow* and WOW times a million – I felt Seb *kiss* me on the cheek. (*Blam!* went another flash.)

Less than 24 hours later, with only a few splinters piercing the skin of my fingers from wrestling open my bedroom window, I could *still* feel the hair on the back of my neck tingle at the memory of that kiss. (But then, how could I forget it, when it was my first ever – from a boy, I mean, and not a parent, little brother or elderly relative?)

And as I sat perched on the window of my shambles of a bedroom – staring out at the tangle of weeds and rubble that was supposed to be our back garden, across jumbled cottage rooftops towards the sea where the gulls cawed and screeched – all I wanted was to be able to go back one, single, *solitary* day and re-live it all again. But not as shy Stella; oh, no. I'd love to be a different Stella altogether, Stella the star, who smiled confidently at Seb and said, "Well, I've always thought you were kind of cute too!" And then *everything* could have been different. Maybe he'd have gone on to declare his undying love for me and we'd have spent the summer zapping off e-mail love letters and planning trips to visit each other.

But, oops . . . I wasn't that Stella. *I* was the sort of Stella who ends up sitting in a smelly room all alone on a Saturday night with splinters in her fingers and without even a *photo* of Seb for company. Good grief, Frankie had gone to all the trouble of getting him to sign the Polaroid last night without me knowing, and now I couldn't find even a crumpled, torn *corner* of it anywhere in this mess of a house.

Urgh. I was in serious danger of being blue. Time to do something. Maybe I should write a list; here was a pen, here was a scrap of cardboard torn off the side of one of my boxes. . .

Things I'm going to like about Portbay:
• calling it Portbore
• seeing the *You Are Now Leaving Portbay!* sign when we're going back to London on visits

Things I'm going to miss about Kentish Town (in no particular order):
• our flat
• my room
• groovy Camden Market just down the road
• the no. 134 bus that takes you all the way into the West End for Saturday shopping trips
• Clive, our mad neighbour, who likes flinging his windows open and singing Frank Sinatra songs at the top of his (very high) voice
• Hampstead Heath being practically on the

doorstep
- drooling over Seb in the corridors at school
- all my noisy, funny gang
- Frankie (of course)
- and not forgetting Aunt Esme. . .

Oops – maybe the list was a bad idea. It was making me homesick, not happier.

"Stella, my sweetheart, when things are getting you down, what've you got to do?"

"Do something nice!" I'd smile at Aunt Esme, who was also known as Aunt Mummy for a while when I was first learning to talk. (Mum was a bit hurt by that, but considering Aunt Esme was my childminder and I saw more of her during the week than Mum it was no big surprise, really.)

"That's right, my sweetheart – do something nice!" she'd beam proudly at me, as if she was a teacher and I was her Stella-the-star pupil.

Aunt Esme (not my real aunt, but Frankie's real mum), is *big* on catchphrases. She's also a very big lady, which is lovely when you're a little kid and getting a squashy hug from her. (Or a tearful 13 year old getting a hug when you're leaving London for ever. . .)

"You know, the quiet ones are often the wise

ones!" she'd sometimes whisper to me when I was younger, as I sat silently but happily at her kitchen table, drawing wobbly flowers and blobby cats. "Not like my Francesca, God bless her!"

And then she'd smile benevolently at Frankie, who'd be doing something manic like running around the room at top speed and top volume, pretending to be a fire engine.

Well, I might be living on another planet as from today (Planet Portbore), but all of a sudden I could practically *hear* Aunt Esme's words booming into my ears right now.

Yep, it was time I tried to do something nice.

And so I unpacked my big red plastic box of art stuff and flipped open the lid, staring at the mouthwatering shades of coloured chalk pencils in there (they're kind of expensive, but my favourite thing to draw with). I Blu-tacked up the caricature I'd done of Neisha and Lauren for the school art show last term (I got a credit for it, but Lauren went a bit huffy and said I'd made her look like a Vulcan. I don't think she *gets* that caricatures aren't *meant* to be pretty). I Blu-tacked up my favourite pictures of me and Frankie: a strip of cheesy photo-booth snaps with both of us – OK, Frankie – fooling around. I set out all my leaving presents on the top of my chest of drawers, and held up the necklace Lauren had given me, sniffed the Body Shop gift set from Parminder, smiled at Eleni's home-made compilation CD ("It's all our favourite singles from the last year!") and smiled even more at the hip-hop CD from Neisha (she'd never managed it yet, but she was *still* trying to convert me to all the music *she* liked!). And then there were the posh Rotring art pens from Frankie ("So you can do caricatures of all your NEW friends when you forget about us!!" she'd joked in her card.)

But even though it all got me smiling, none of it really cheered me up, not deep down. And none of it could distract me from the terrible *pong* in here. . .

Except the smells in my smelly room weren't the same any more, I suddenly noticed. The breeze from outside had wafted in, replacing the cardboard, damp, Dettol and puke pongs with . . . what exactly? There was the sea (sort of salty), something a bit whiffy, like cabbage (seaweed, I sussed out) and something much nicer. Was it flowery, like honeysuckle, or jasmine? No – it was more like . . . like peaches and cream, weirdly enough. Where was *that* coming from? Dumbly, I glanced outside the window, though I didn't know what I was supposed to be looking for. A great big pudding lorry passing by, maybe? But all I could see – apart from our weedy, so-called garden and the rooftops and the swirling gulls – was one fat, scruffy ginger cat, wobbling its way precariously along the top of the garden fence, like a high-wire walker at the circus (who's eaten too many burgers for lunch lately).

"Hee hee hee!"

Please no!

"Hee hee hee!"

Surely there was some mistake; *surely* I hadn't missed a toddler-waking volcano in the last few minutes. The only thing that didn't freeze at the sound of that giggle was my heart, which collapsed down to my stomach with total *dread*. In my family, in the last couple of years at least, I'd learned that a "Hee hee hee!" like that meant only one thing: trouble. No, make that *TROUBLE*.

I spun my head around quick enough to give me whiplash and instantly saw Jamie practising his biting skills on one of my chalk pencils, while snapping another in half as he doodled a toddler's impression of the devil (probably) on my bedroom wall.

Good grief, were my little brothers determined to make this miserable house move just that *bit* more unbearable for me?

There was only one thing that could keep me sane at the moment – the thought that in seven days' time, Frankie would be coming for the weekend (yes, yes, YES!). That's if my family didn't drive me so mad beforehand that I'd be on the verge of stowing myself on the first train back to Kentish Town.

But maybe I'd reached boiling point already. As I watched Jamie pull the cobalt-blue chalk pencil out of his mouth and snap *that* in half too, I felt something snap inside of *me*.

"G-g-g-g-g-get out of my room, n-n-n-n-*NOW*, J-J-J-Jamie!!"

Ah, I *wondered* when my stupid stammer would show up.

Now *there* was something I wouldn't have minded leaving far, far behind in London. . .

Chapter 4

The psycho seagull and other weirdos

"Hey, Lou-Lou!"

Over the top of the huge cardboard box we were both delving into this morning, Mum shot me a knowing look. Dad normally always called her "Louise", and saved "Lou-Lou" for the times he needed to suck up to her *big*-time, like when he'd broken something, or spent daft amounts of cash on a flash new DVD player or whatever.

"Listen, is it OK if I leave you girls to do the unpacking for a little while?" Dad smiled, sticking his blond-haired head around the paint-peeling kitchen doorway. "I thought I should try and get the computer up and running. . ."

Dad. If it hadn't been for his heart attack, we wouldn't be here. Not in the *kitchen*, I mean, in Portbore. And not that he actually *had* a heart attack – but Dad didn't know that at the time, not when he was stuck in a packed tube train on the way home from work a few months ago and managed to terrify everyone in the carriage, as well as himself, by collapsing with chest pains.

It turned out that it was just a panic attack (phew). But after getting told by the hospital that his heart was in tip-top shape, Dad *still* didn't look very well *or* very happy. Mum didn't look too great either, and I kept coming across them having these intense, whispered conversations that (hey, funnily enough) stopped dead when I walked into the room.

A week later, they let me in on their little secret – we were moving.

"Your dad's job's been very stressful for years now," Mum had tried to explain at the time. "He – well, *we* – feel like we need a complete change. Somewhere with a slower pace of life. More relaxed."

I think I should remind Mum about what she said back then. She didn't look particularly relaxed as she stopped unravelling plates from old newspapers and glanced up darkly at Dad just now. You'd think he'd just told her that he was off to read the *Beano* or watch *Hollyoaks* or some other total skive like that.

"Andy, it's not very easy to look after the boys *and* do the unpacking by myself!" Mum grumbled, keeping one eye on Jamie and Jake, who were taking turns putting a cardboard box on each other's heads and hitting it.

"But *I'm* helping you, Mum!" I chipped in. "And anyway, we *should* be on-line in case . . . in case Auntie V or someone from Dad's old work needs to get in touch!"

Ha! Auntie V might use e-mail in her office, but she'd never sent *us* one. Her style was to yak on the phone, or round the dining table in our old flat, for hours at a time. And why would anyone from Dad's old work e-mail a) on a Sunday, and b) at all? What would they say? "Andy Stansfield – you are stark, raving mad for giving up a highly paid job as an accountant for a posh magazine company, and dragging your entire family down to a faded seaside resort where you've got no work and a just pile of mouldy bricks to live in!"

"Fine! Fix up the computer, then!" Mum sighed, pushing her layered, dark-brown hair back from her face.

"Oh . . . OK!" Dad shrugged and smiled, then disappeared before guilt got the better of him and he found himself roped into deciding which cupboard to stack the tins in, or distracting the twins long enough to stop them from giving each other concussion.

Of course, the *real* reason I wanted Dad to get the computer set up was so that I could e-mail Frankie and all the rest of my friends. I adore e-mail. No, I don't just adore it, I *adoooorrrrre* it. Texting is OK for stuff like: *Hi, how r u?*, but there's no room for waffling, is there? E-mail is when I get the chance to be as funny and fluent as my friends are out loud.

Out loud is something I have a problem with, if you haven't picked up on that already.

While we're (sort of) on the subject, here are two facts:

1) You're more likely to stammer when you're feeling very shy (or very wound-up).

2) The letter "S" is one of the hardest letters to say when you're prone to stammering.

So it's just my luck to be a) horribly shy, and b) called Stella Stansfield. Imagine how difficult *that* is to say when you're nervous and meeting people for the first time, like when you've moved to a new town, for example. . .

"But Stella, you're lucky that your stammer isn't *too* bad," Auntie V suggested to me once, over the dining-room table. "It's not as though you have it all the time. It's not like that young singer boy Gary what's-his-name."

No, I wasn't as bad as *Gareth* Gates used to be (Auntie V met him at an after-show party for some musical a couple of years or so ago). And I certainly wasn't as bad as people I'd seen in documentaries, who struggled with every sentence, every minute of the day. My stammer only crept up on me now and again, but I guess the *fear* of it creeping up was what made me keep words locked up in my head instead of coming out of my mouth a lot of the time.

"RAAAAARGHHHH!"

"AAAAAARGHHHH!"

Still, the constant noise booming from both my brothers *more* than made up for the lack of noise on *my* part. Today's "RAAAAARGHH!" came from Jamie, who'd just found an old, wooden dust-brush in the crumbling kitchen fireplace and was now thudding it off the top of the cardboard box containing Jake's head. The echoey-sounding "AAAAAARGHHHH!" was Jake trying to let Jamie know that their game had gone too far.

"Stella," my mum looked at me wearily. "Could you be the most fantastic daughter in the world and stop your brothers from killing each other before I parcel-tape them both to the legs of the kitchen table? *Please?*"

I did more than just stop Jake and Jamie from killing each other: I hustled the twins out of the back door and into the garden.

"What will we play?" I tried asking them, knowing that football was out, since there was no such thing as a flat piece of grass or earth out here. Course, we could always play *Hunt* the Football. . . I could turn around and chuck the ball over my shoulder into the overgrown jungle of weed-beds and mutant shrubs, and then we could pass a pleasant week or two trying to find it amongst all that matted foliage.

"CHASE!" yelled Jake, and immediately hurled himself into the greenery, with a roaring Jamie in hot pursuit.

In two seconds flat, all I could see of them was their heads (one fair, one strawberry-blond) bobbing about as they roared and ran. If either of them went down on all fours, I'd end up playing Hunt the *Twin*.

"Prrrrp!"

Hmm. That small sound I heard above (or in spite of) the racket Jamie and Jake were making . . . what was it?

"Prrrrp!"

Maybe we had crickets in our garden (hey, we

could have had a family of sabre-toothed tigers living in that tangle and never know it).

"Prrrrp!"

But it wasn't coming from anywhere in the garden exactly; the "prrrrp" seemed to be prrrrping from an ugly, broken-down brick shed thing over by the right-hand wall. I took two steps closer to it, stumbling over a broken flowerpot and a dented plastic watering can camouflaged in the knee-high spiky grass.

The brick shed had a weather-tattered wooden door and one small window, consisting of three panes of solid dust (that I supposed had *glass* lurking behind it) and one empty space framed by dangerous-looking shards twinkling in the sunlight.

And inside . . . inside I could see something.

Something moving.

A flurry of orange fur slinking around.

My brain flipped from PANIC! (i.e. unidentified-moving-object-that-MIGHT-be-a-sabre-toothed-tiger) to AHA! (i.e. maybe-*probably*-it's-that-fat-cat-I-saw-last-night) to PANIC! again, at the sound of my little brothers' matching screams. . .

"Isn't shingles some kind of horrible skin disease?"

I whispered to Mum, as I squinted at the name stamped in the corner of all the serviettes.

We were sitting in the window seat of a seafront café – me, Mum and my muppety brothers.

"*Yes*, but I think this place is called the Shingle café not the *Shingles* café and it's probably named after the shingle on the beach, don't you, Stella?"

Mum raised her eyebrows, knowing I was deliberately looking on the black side. (Unlike her, gazing at everything in this town through rose-tinted specs.)

Shingle/Shingles, Portbay/Portbore; whatever . . . anyway I'm *sure* the other customers in the café moved their chairs away from us when we walked in, and I wouldn't have blamed them for thinking Jamie was contagious with something gross like shingles. After all, how could they know that the red rash all over his face and arms was 'cause of him running head-first into a nettle patch, and that his bloodshot eyes were only like that 'cause of the sand that Jake had kicked into them on the beach ten minutes ago?

"Ooh! Lovely! Thank you!" Mum suddenly smiled, as the most sullen waitress in the world wordlessly thunked plates of beans and fish fingers down in front of the twins.

I didn't dare to stare, but I couldn't help noticing that the tall, skinny girl currently splattering us with bean juice had the same colour hair as the sabre-toothed tiger/ginger cat in our shed this morning. Unfortunately for her, her red hair clashed badly with her bright pink face. Maybe she'd just had a row with her boss. Or maybe she just hated customers. Or maybe she had the first signs of shingles. . .

Anyway, with a name like a skin condition and a waitress as "welcoming" as that, it was a mystery why there were so many mugs (like us) hanging out in the Shingles café. Maybe the old people I could see were lucky enough to be just visiting (we'd passed a car park stuffed with tour buses), and maybe all the teenagers were here because it was the only café in town and there was nothing much *else* to do in Portbore on the first weekend of the summer holidays (it wouldn't surprise me).

The reason *we* were having our lunch in this dump with a dodgy name was because Mum had given up any attempt at unpacking after my brothers had managed to puncture themselves in our lethal garden. Leaving Dad alone in peace to play on – er, *set up* – the computer, Mum had announced that me, her and the boys were going to the beach, where hopefully Jamie and Jake would tear around in the sand and keep out of danger for once in their tiny lives.

"Isn't the prom beautiful?" Mum beamed, gazing out of the window.

She'd just pushed the regular cutlery away from Jake's inquisitive fingers and given him (and Jamie) a yellow plastic Mothercare set that she always took with her when we went out to eat with my brothers. (I think she was wary of letting Jake near any sharp objects after he speared his leg on the rusty old garden fork this morning.)

"It's OK," I shrugged in reply to Mum's comment, wondering what was so beautiful about a pavement and some painted blue railings. Anyway, I could hardly see the prom – or the sea or the beach beyond it – for coaches of day-tripping OAPs trundling by.

"It was so pretty last night, the way all the lights strung along here flickered on just as it started to get dark!"

Yeah, and it was so pretty the way Jamie was smearing tomato sauce all over his face with his hands while Mum wasn't looking. I took the last two serviettes out of their metal holder and tried to daub the worst of the red gunk off him.

"NO!!" Jamie yelled, shoving me away. (Gee, *thanks*.)

"Last night, me and your dad were talking about how peaceful it is here," said Mum cheerfully, as she turned round and took over wiping-duty from me. "It's not exactly like strolling down Kentish Town High Street on a Saturday night, is it?"

I knew what Mum was getting at. Round the tube station in Kentish Town, these down-and-out guys hung out, drinking tins of lager. The local paper liked to bang on about drug-dealing going on in the area. And even though our neighbour, Clive, never did anything nuts apart from warbling Frank Sinatra hits out his window, I think Mum always had her Weirdo Alert on when it came to him. (Poor bloke.)

Well, fair enough – so I didn't know if there were down-and-outs or any drug-dealing problems in Portbore (probably not), but there's one thing for sure: big cities aren't the only place you get weirdos. In the hour we'd spent mucking about on the beach, I'd seen three total weirdos already: some batty old dear sitting on a bench, feeding candyfloss to a ginger *cat*, for goodness' sake (a furry relative of the puss hanging out in our garden, maybe?); a young lad hopping around on the sand like he had itching powder in his boxer shorts (he *was* being dive-bombed by a psycho seagull, though); and some mad-looking Goth girl kicking her way grumpily through the sand in Doc Marten boots, a black leather jacket and – wait for it – a pink *tutu*.

Help – I'd moved to Portbore, the seaside resort for loonies of all ages (and species)...

"Oh, I forgot to tell you!" Mum suddenly said, while holding Jake's legs down to stop him from kicking Jamie. "Me and your dad saw a poster last night – there's a funfair coming to town on Friday. You could take Frankie when she comes at the weekend – it'll be brilliant!"

OK, so funfairs are fun. But they're hardly "brilliant" – not when you've been to Chessington World of Adventures (eight times, as me and Frankie have clocked up). And a big wheel is a laugh to go on, but it's not exactly the London Eye (me and Frankie have been on that twice, once with Auntie Esme for Frankie's birthday, and once with school).

"Mmm..." I mumbled non-committally to Mum, hoping she didn't think I was being all awkward and negative again.

But she hadn't even noticed my "Mmm. . ." because Jamie had got Jake back for kicking him by scoring a direct hit with a major squirt from the ketchup bottle.

"Jamie – *NO!* Stella, can you please go and grab some more paper napkins? Oh! Jamie – now *DON'T* bite your brother. . .!"

Before the inevitable screams and wails broke out, I got up and sped off towards the counter to grab a handful of "Shingles"-printed serviettes from the teetering pile stacked there. It *should* have been one of those nothingy, ten-second chores, but somehow the search-for-the-serviette turned into a not-so-mini trauma for me.

"Um. . ."

I'd just nipped past a couple of tables of gossiping OAPs when I nearly tripped over a pair of long legs stretched out between two chairs. I kind of hoped that "um. . ." would do: that the owner of the long legs (one of four prissily perfect girls around my age) would see that she was barring my way and reel her legs in to let me by. Instead, the legs stayed put, giving their owner – and her buddies – plenty of time to look me up, down and back again. Call me paranoid, but you could tell they didn't like what they saw. So I had on a white T-shirt, a denim mini, stripy socks and a pair of trainers – so what? I mean, next to my super-trendy friends back in Kentish Town, I probably looked *frumpy*. But here in dullsville Portbore, I must have looked like Kate Moss trying too hard, all because . . . because of what? My stripy pastel socks? *That's* what the four of them were scowling at. Hey, I only bought them because I'd seen them in *Mizz* last month and thought they were kind of cute. . .

"'S-s-s-s-scuse me. . ."

Here we go. Here came my stammer, all because of some stupid tomato sauce, a stupid serviette, and some stupid, *stupid*, stripy socks.

I didn't stick around long enough to listen to whether or not the girls were sniggering at me tripping over my words (like some people at my old school had, before Frankie stepped in and made sure they didn't giggle *again*). I just saw that the legs had withdrawn and that my path to the counter was clear – so I hurried over, grabbed a few serviettes, then swivelled round and headed back by a different route. All I wanted was to skirt past a few tables of happy pensioners and get safely back to Mum and the twins and the uninspiring view of the prom that Mum had been wittering on about.

Uh-oh.

It wasn't that easy. On my *new* route, I had to pass a table of boys a couple of years older than me – about 15, I reckoned from a split-second shy glance – and *then* I heard it.

"Check the hair!" one of them said.

"Yeah, pure afro!" said one of the others.

My hair . . . you can describe it in a lot of ways: "practically blonde!" (that's Frankie, who thinks anything less than black or dark brown is practically blonde), to "curly-wurly" (Jake), to "ringlety" (Auntie V), to "like an angel's!" (Aunt Esme). But the thing is, if you're going to get technical about my practically blonde (i.e. light brown), curly-wurly, ringlety, "angelic" hair, it *is* – technically speaking – afro. How come that lad had managed to make a simple fact sound like an insult?

"Hey, and check the boobs!" I heard another of the boys cackle, before a bluster of other cacklers joined in.

This was *too* much. I felt like the Number One Freak in a Victorian freak show.

Blushing, *mortified*, I couldn't get back to Mum, Jake and Jamie fast enough. And then – I couldn't believe it – Mum started giggling too.

"Oh, dear – I think you might need to change that top when we get home!" she laughed, pointing at my chest.

I gazed down at my white T-shirt, and clocked the tomato-sauce handprints pressed *straight* on to my boobs.

"Thanks, Jamie!" I grumbled darkly, as my little brother happily giggled to himself, squirting tomato sauce down his shorts.

"I need some air," I told Mum, as I headed for the door, not even bothering to sit down (and get covered with *more* ketchup in embarrassing places).

What I *really* needed, I realized – once I was outside in the fresh, coach-exhaust-scented air – was my friends. So how come no one (except Frankie, yesterday, briefly) had answered any of my phone calls or texts this weekend. . .?

Chapter 5

Four quarters of me

"Oh, Stella! Don't do *that*!" Mum sighed, as she walked back into the bathroom with the boys' clean pyjamas.

"What?" I asked innocently. "Don't you think they look cute?"

Jake and Jamie seemed to like the soapy devil horns I'd shaped their soft baby hair into – they couldn't stop snickering at the sight of each other.

"And couldn't you have stopped them from emptying half the bath-water on to the floor? Look at the state of this carpet!"

I think Mum realized how dumb that sounded almost straight away. For a start, trying to get Jamie and Jake to stop doing something naughty was as hard as juggling custard. And as for the faded, stained old rag of a carpet in this mouldy, damp room, it could probably do with a good wash anyway. Actually, it could probably do with being ripped up and shoved in the skip that was being delivered in the morning. (Dad was supposed to be starting on the house renovations tomorrow, but the only thing I'd heard him threaten to throw in the skip so far was the computer he'd been trying to get working for the last eight hours. . .)

"Right – this little monster's mine," said Mum, rinsing the suds out of the devil horns of the nearest dripping, giggling small boy (who happened to be Jamie, while I got the noisy, roaring one – Jake – who at least didn't bite) and scooping him up.

"Did you manage to get hold of Frankie yet?"

"No," I told Mum, as I did the same to Jake and then clamped my knees like a vice around his ankles to keep him semi-still while I wrapped a big fluffy towel around him. "Aunt Esme said she was out with the girls again."

Aunt Esme had also been a bit surprised, like me, that Frankie hadn't returned the two messages and three texts I'd sent her today.

"Well, you two'll have plenty of catching up to do next weekend anyway, and I'm *sure* Frankie'll have lots of messages from Lauren and everyone!" Mum smiled brightly, as if she could tell I wasn't too happy with the big fat wall of silence from most of my friends since Friday night.

I was *trying* not to let that get me down. After

all, it had only been two days, which might have seemed like a week past *for ever* for me, stuck down here at the edge of the world, but probably felt like about ten *minutes* to Frankie and the others. And I really *was* looking forward to Frankie coming; I couldn't wait to pour my heart out to her about stuff like missing Seb and the embarrassment of what had happened in the café this lunchtime. I tell you, those lads wouldn't dare make *any* kind of comment to Frankie, not if they wanted to live. One ferocious glance from her and they'd be *whimpering*.

"You're not still bugged by what those boys said at the café today, are you?" Mum suddenly quizzed me, reading my mind again. (Wish she'd been able to read my mind better the last few months when I'd been silently yelling, "Don't make me move away!!")

"A bit," I shrugged, rubbing the now soapless, wet-look horns – and a whole shower of wet sand – out of Jake's hair with the towel.

"But when people don't know you, Stella, they'll always pick up on what's unusual about you at first. They don't necessarily *mean* anything by it."

I knew that. My favourite thing to draw was caricatures, wasn't it? And with caricatures, you have to fix on just a few features and exaggerate them. But hypocritical as it might sound, I didn't want anyone "fixing" on what made *me* different. And I wasn't just talking about my hair or my stripy socks or the tomato-sauce handprints across my boobs. What worried me was that here in Portbore, I could tell that our whole *family* was going to seem unusual. Mainly 'cause we look like we aren't even *related* to each other. It's like we all drew straws and just ended up together by accident. I mean, the twins don't even look like *twins*, for goodness' sake. Actually, if I was drawing caricatures of my family, *here's* what I'd pick out. . .

DAD: Tall, short blond hair, blue eyes. (Looks Norwegian, but is actually from Norfolk.)

MUM: Layered dark-brown hair that regularly flops across her face, olive skin, big brown eyes. (Looks Spanish, but is from Hackney, East London.)

JAKE: Short, dumpy, fluffily spiky fair hair, grey eyes. (Looks like Grandpa Stansfield's mini-me.)

JAMIE: Tall for his age, skinny, ultra-pale skin, strawberry-blond wavy hair. (Just like the photos we've seen of Mum's mum – Nana Jones.)

Then there's me. The four quarters that make

up Stella Stansfield (i.e. the genes from all my grandparents) somehow add up to something different from the rest of my family. I ended up with light-brown fizzy ringlets, hazel eyes, and a smattering of freckles right across my nose (like a brush loaded with coffee-coloured paint got flicked my way at point-blank range). No one can figure out where the freckles came from (none of my grandparents are guilty of freckles), but the hair is easy. That's 'cause one quarter of me is from Norfolk, one quarter of me is from Yorkshire, one quarter of me is cockney – and one quarter is from Barbados.

"How come *you* don't look more like your dad?" I asked Mum, though I knew the answer already – I'd asked the question before.

"Sometimes genes can skip a generation," Mum shrugged. "I mean, my skin's darker than yours, which must have come from my father. But you don't see your lovely hair as a problem, do you, Stella?"

I shook my head. I *liked* my curls, apart from the amount of time I had to spend conditioning them, and having stupid, ignorant dorks in cafés sniggering at them, of course.

"I wish I could see a picture of my grandad. . ."

I sighed. I'd said that before, plenty of times, too. I also wished I could've met Nana Jones in person, but I didn't happen to get born till years after she died.

"I know, Stella. But like I've said already, I only ever saw one photo of my father when I was a little girl, and I don't know what happened to it."

How weird: the idea that Nana Jones and this boy fell in love with each other when she was only four years older than I am now – but she didn't dare tell her parents, just 'cause he was black. And how weird that I knew so little about him. In fact, apart from that stuff, I only knew four things about my grandad: 1) he was kind, 2) he was handsome, 3) his name was Eddie, and 4) he'd come from Barbados to live in Britain with his parents when he was just a little boy. Not much to know about a grandparent, is it?

"Remember, it *was* a very long time ago, Stella, and people's attitudes were very different back then," said Mum, doing that unsettling thing again, as if she could read my mind. "They were ignorant about colour, and they were ignorant about things like expecting babies when you weren't married."

And all that long time ago, my grandad left London broken-hearted because Nana Jones split up with him, scared of what her parents thought.

And here's the saddest thing about the whole mega-sad thing: he never knew that he was going to be a dad . . . and one day a grandad, to me and the Muppets.

"How did Nana Jones meet Grandad Eddie again?" I quizzed Mum, trying to piece the story together in my head.

"He was working in Hackney for the summer, and don't ask me what his job was, 'cause I don't remember my mother ever mentioning it."

"Where do you think he could be now?" I asked her, leaning over and grabbing Jake before he managed to clamber back into the noisily draining bath.

"Well, if he's still alive, he could be anywhere in the world, couldn't he? I mean, he could have retired back to Barbados, or even be living two miles from here!" said Mum, as she tried to stop Jamie from ramming both feet down one leg of his Fimbles pyjamas. "There's just no way of ever knowing, Stella – specially since it all happened nearly forty years ago now, and we don't even know his last name."

My mum's amazingly practical. I don't mean that in a horrible way; she just has this talent for not freaking about stuff that you can't do anything about. And she's also got a talent for sorting stuff that you *can* do something about, which is, I guess, why she made Dad move here before he had any more panic attacks and frightened *more* passengers on the tube. . .

"Jake – *leave* the soap!" Mum suddenly ordered, reaching over and prising a bar of Simple out from between his stubby white teeth. "You saw what happened to Jamie last night. Do you want to end up being sick too?"

"YES!" trumpeted Jake.

I hadn't even noticed what he'd been up to. For a second there, my thoughts had drifted back to my old school, where everyone was white, black, Asian, Jewish, Turkish and Greek-Cypriot; where loads of pupils came from Croatia and Afghanistan and Korea and Somalia and a load of other countries you might struggle to place on a map of the world. Back there, it hadn't mattered one bit that my family didn't quite match, or that one quarter of me was from a grandad I'd never seen. All that my friends cared about was the fact that my parents worked on magazines (at least, Mum did till she had the twins) and they reckoned that was very, *very* cool indeed.

But now . . . well, now I guess I was a bit worried that in Portbore, we'd just be the Weird

Family From London. Er, exactly *how* were we supposed to feel at home here. . .?

The teeth-marks were still throbbing on my arm as I headed to my bedroom. (That was the *last* time I offered to read my brothers a bedtime story – I didn't care if Jamie was only acting out the part of *The Hungry Caterpillar*.)

I needed to speak to Frankie; after the freaky day I'd had I needed to feel like me, and not some fizzy-haired alien who'd landed by the seaside.

And then there it was again . . . a waft of peaches and cream, floating above the smells of baby talc and foam bath lingering up my nostrils. I meant to hurry over to my window and look outside again – to figure out where the waft was wafting from – when I stopped dead.

Things might still be in a muddle in my room (like the rest of the house), but I *definitely* would have remembered unpacking a huge, fat, tatty, ginger cat. The one currently snoring its scruffy head off on my bed did *not* belong to me.

"Um . . . hello? Puss-puss, do you want to go back where you belong?" I said, shooing it warily from a safe distance. (I didn't like the look of those battle-scarred ears – it could probably beat me in a fight.)

The cat, probably sensing that I was zero threat to it, snored on – one lethal-looking yellow fang protruding from its dreamily quivering mouth.

"Did you come in through the window, puss?" I asked it, taking a tentative step closer and wondering how I was going to persuade it to go back *out* the window.

The cat, blanking me again, gave a reverberating sigh and stretched itself into a relaxed arc, that practically took up half the width of my bed. (*Was* it a direct descendant of a south coast sabre-toothed tiger?)

And then I saw something *else* I hadn't seen in my room last time I'd looked.

Gently, gently, I took a corner of the brightly coloured leaflet poking out from under the cat's furry white belly and *pulled*.

All the Fun of the Fair! In Portbay from Friday!

Before I got a chance to figure out how the fairground flyer had got here, I got the strangest shivery feeling I was being watched – from one menacing, green, feline eye.

"Frankie?" I whispered into my mobile, as her message service clicked in. "You'd better get here quick. *Everything* about this town is freaking me out. . .!"

Chapter 6

Fairy cakes and sardines

"Good grief, Stella: you've made me look like a meerkat. Crossed with a heron. Wearing very expensive shoes!"

That was the first and last time I'd done a caricature of Auntie V – she'd popped around to our old flat after work one day, and settled herself down at the dining table for one of her regular catch-ups with my parents. She always looks pretty stunning, my Auntie V, 'cause like my dad, she's tall ("these could have been dancer's legs, Stella, darling!") and blonde ("I'd have made a better Roxy in *Chicago* than that Renée Zellweger!"). *Unlike* my dad, Auntie V is totally into exploiting her fake Nordic look, and never dresses in anything but shades of white, cream and fawn, with deep red lipstick and piles of ethnic jewellery ("for a bit of drama, darling!"). Anyway, that particular time, I'd drawn her all elongated and glamorous, from the top of her sharp blonde bob to her pointy camel-coloured ankle boots. I'd been really pleased with it. Auntie V seemed as pleased as if I'd spilt Ribena over her white angora jersey.

"You're obviously very good at drawing, Stella, darling. But why don't you try another style? Why don't you draw something pretty for a change, like flowers or fruit, etc., etc.?"

And now, sitting on a bench on the prom, with my pad in front of me and a chalk pencil in one hand, I suddenly remembered what Auntie V had said that day, however long ago. And the reason I didn't draw flowers, fruit, etc., etc. (Auntie V talked very fast – I think she liked to say "etc." just to save time) was because I was rotten at drawing them. Just like I was rotten at drawing beaches, as I was finding out.

"Stupid sea, stupid sky, stupid caravans. . ." I grumbled to myself, staring off at the ugly jumble of metal boxes perched up on the headland, and then back down at the just-as-ugly boxy blobs I'd scribbled on to the paper. The only thing I liked about my picture was the seagull standing on the prom railing, watching every reluctant stroke of my pencil, and probably hoping I might have half a doughnut or something that I'd like to share with it. I'd drawn the bird with a big crooked beak, crossed eyes and finned feet as big as clown's shoes. But somehow, my cute caricature of the gull didn't fit too well with the atmospheric landscape I wasn't managing to capture. At all.

I felt like grabbing my darkest red chalk pencil from the box and swirling mad, bad, ugly doodles over the whole thing. But then I *was* in a Gold Star Grouch this morning; *everything* was hacking me off. OK, so I'd had my first good night's sleep since I got here – the snoring of the cat-I-was-too-scared-to-move had been kind of soothing (it reminded me of the sound of cars swooshing by at all hours in Kentish Town). But then I got woken up at 7.30 a.m. this morning by the ear-splitting, metallic KERR-*LAAANNNGG* of a skip being delivered in our driveway. (The cat, by the way, was nowhere to be seen – back to wherever it had come from, I supposed. But I still had the flyer for the funfair, wherever *that* had come from.)

Anyway, first there was the KERR-*LAAANNNGG*, and then two seconds later, I had a couple of over-excited small boys bouncing up and down on my bed (with me still in it), yelling "Skip! SKIP! SKIPPP!!!" at the tops of their voices. Dad was *also* very excited by the arrival of the skip (but at least he didn't show it by jumping on my bed); in fact, he was *so* excited that he'd decided he was having a day off from struggling with the computer. Which meant yet again, no e-mails for me.

"Look, it's Monday, so the library will be open. Why don't you see if it's got any computers you could check your e-mails on? Or you could go into town and see if there's an internet café somewhere!" Mum had suggested, when she saw the black cloud of gloom hovering over my head at breakfast. "You could take your pad out with you and do some drawing. It's a beautiful day!"

I had a hunch that Portbore was so behind the times that they'd only just got Channel 5 on the telly, never mind anything as radical as an internet connection (maybe *that* was why Dad couldn't get the computer to work). And I wasn't really in the mood to dig out my chalk pencils. But faced with a choice of watching Dad play at Chucking-Things-in-the-Skip, helping Mum unpack saucepans, or acting as unpaid zookeeper to the Muppets, I decided I might as well take up Mum's offer and escape.

So far, I hadn't bothered to go and look for non-existent computers, but I was seriously considering a new way to pass the time – turning this rubbish drawing of mine into an origami boat and sailing it out to sea. . .

"Oooh, *that's* lovely, dear!"

There was a light thunk on the bench beside me and the sweet smell of toffee as a very old lady settled herself down to inspect my artwork. Despite the baking sun, she was wearing a lime green raincoat and had a pink meringue of a hat on her head.

"It's not really," I shrugged.

"Oh, but it is, dear. Toffee?"

She flipped open a catch on her cream patent-leather handbag and pulled out a rustling bag of sweets. I wasn't sure what to do – in London, you don't tend to get chatting to strangers and you certainly don't go taking Werther's Originals off them. But this lady was hardly a child-snatching psycho – she was about a hundred and twelve, and if she tried anything funny I could just pull her meringue down over her face and scarper.

"Um, thanks. . ." I said warily, helping myself to one of her sweets.

"Good enough for the window of the gallery on the prom. Do you know it?" she asked, unwrapping a toffee for herself.

"Er, no," I mumbled, self-consciously flipping my ropey picture over and finding myself with a blank white sheet (*big* improvement).

The bag of toffee went back in her tiny bag, and instead she pulled out a fairy cake, complete with a pleated paper cup and a cherry on top. She gave it a quick blow, sending a few specks of fluff fluttering into the breeze.

"It's his favourite." She nodded at the gull, which – right on cue – swooped down to her feet, waiting patiently for its treat. "Just here on holiday, are you?"

"No – just moved. To Foxglove Cottage, up on Dingle Lane."

God, I *hated* my new address – it sounded so *cutesy*. (Apart from that, what the heck was a foxglove supposed to look like anyway? And what was a dingle when it was at home?) You know, I hated my new address so much that I hadn't *dared* tell Neisha what it was yet; she was so into Eminem and hardcore hip-hop that I thought she'd laugh in my face for living somewhere that sounded like it was just next door to the Teletubbies.

"Ah, yes. It used to be lovely, that cottage."

"My dad's doing it up," I told her. (Ha! I was looking forward to *that* – the closest my dad had ever got to DIY in the past was ringing people up under the DIY section in the *Yellow Pages*.)

"And where have you moved from, dear?"

"London. North London. Kentish Town."

As I watched the old lady lean forward and feed crumbs of fairy cake to this pterodactyl of a bird, I gently began tap-tapping my pencil on the edge of the blank sheet of paper. And then I started drawing.

"London? Ooh, I went up there once for a day trip," the old lady chattered. "Meant to go to Buckingham Palace to have a look at the Queen, but I got terribly muddled with those tube trains and ended up at a place called Walthamstow Dog Track. Do you know it?"

"Well, yes," I frowned at the top of her bobbing, pink-hatted head, wondering how she'd managed to get *that* lost. "That's where they hold greyhound races. I went with my dad once. Did you get to Buckingham Palace in the end?" I talked and scribbled at the same time, the caricature coming to me a *hundred* times easier than the landscape had five minutes ago.

"Oh, no. Someone showed me how the betting worked, and I stayed and won £5 on a greyhound called Boozy Bessie. Had a lovely afternoon!

Ah . . . it must seem quite quiet around here after London, dear."

"I guess so," I agreed with her, quickly scooping two more chalk pencils – one pink and one lime green – from the box by my side.

"Of course, Portbay wasn't *always* quiet. Not back in the old days, when there was all the piracy and smuggling going on."

"Pirates?" I squeaked in surprise. What *was* this place we'd moved to? *Wait* till I told Mum – bloodthirsty pirates and smugglers were pretty heavy-going compared to a few down-and-outs sharing a can of lager and chatting outside the tube station. . .

"And then there's the house in Sugar Bay. It's got a bit of a history to it, that rambling old place," the equally rambling old lady breezed on, as if pirates and smugglers were run-of-the-mill stuff. "Had a walk over there yet, to Sugar Bay?"

"No – where's that?"

"Well, you were nearly drawing it a minute ago!" she smiled, brushing the last of the cake crumbs from her fingers. "It's a beautiful little cove just on the other side of that cliff. Nothing there now but the old house, and those tin cans, of course."

She was pointing up at the caravans teetering

on the headland. Now that it had finished its snack lunch, the seagull hopped up to join the old lady on the bench, and seemed to be staring disapprovingly at the holiday homes too. Maybe it would fly over and poo on them later.

I wanted to ask more, to find out all about the pirates and the smugglers and the old house and what its story was (and how exactly she'd found out that the gull liked fairy cakes best), but the old lady's attention was suddenly grabbed by something else.

"Would you look at him?" she laughed, nodding her wobbly net-swathed hat towards the beach just below us. "You'd think nobody had ever bothered telling him he was a cat!"

Something went ping! in my head as I recognized the fat ginger cat sunbathing on the sand, eyes closed, four furry feet in the air, big belly on show.

"It was in my room last night!" I exclaimed.

"Peaches was? Oh, he gets around. A real wanderer. Settles himself with whoever he fancies for a while, then he's off. He even lived with me once upon a time. Liked custard cream biscuits and sardines, as I remember."

"Peaches?"

I had to make sure I'd heard her properly – that scruffy, battle-scarred, overweight cat *was* called "Peaches", right?

"Yes, Peaches – because of his colouring, I suppose."

Peaches. If I'd have *had* to guess at a name for him, I'd have come up with stuff like Big Ron or Bruiser or Tank or something. Then again, there had been that weird sweet scent in my room all last night. . .

At that second, another ping! went off in my head, as I realized that the old lady I'd been talking to was the same mad one I'd spotted yesterday sharing candyfloss with a cat. And that cat probably *was* Peaches. Wow – it had to be quite a trek on cat-sized legs, getting to the seafront from my house, way up on the slope overlooking town.

"Now what's this you've been up to? Hmm?"

The old lady smiled at me and leant over for a peek at my pad. I was pretty pleased with the sketch, specially since I'd done it so quickly, and flipped it round so she could see it better.

"Oh!" she exclaimed, her pale eyebrows raised. "It's one of those cartoony things. What do you call them again?"

"Caricatures," I told her, scanning her face

to see what she reckoned of it. I'd thought I'd made it quite sweet – like a cross between an old lady and a Neopolitan ice-cream sundae. I'd even drawn a cherry on the top of her hat.

"That's *very* clever," she nodded slowly. "But I've always thought those caricature things are a bit cruel, haven't you? You want to have a go at drawing something pretty. You should have a wander round to Sugar Bay, paint a picture of the old hou—"

I'd never been so glad to hear my phone ring; for one thing, it meant I didn't have to listen to this batty old dear tell me my drawing wasn't very good (just like Auntie V, though you'd never catch *her* in a lime green raincoat and pink meringue hat). And anyway, it could be Frankie – getting back to me at last.

"'Scuse me – I'd better go," I blustered, hurriedly gathering up my art stuff with one hand, and checking out the number calling on the screen of my phone.

Pah . . . only Mum.

"Bye, dear!" the old lady smiled and waved, as I wandered off at high speed.

"Hello, Mum – what's up?" I asked, hoping she was calling me to say that Frankie had phoned the cottage or that Dad had fixed up the computer *after* all and there were *dozens* of messages waiting for me from my friends back in London.

Wrong.

"Hi, Stella – just a quickie. Can you pick up some more milk on the way home? Jake's just poured the last of the litre into my underwear drawer."

And so I wandered back to Foxglove Cottage with a heavy heart (still no word from Frankie), a heavy shopping bag (filled with a carton of milk, a packet of custard creams and a tin of sardines), and a funny, furry ginger shadow following me up every windy lane. . .

Chapter 7

Trapped in Nutsville

It turned out that while Mum was pouring the contents of her knicker drawer (pants, bras, semi-skimmed milk) into the washing machine, Jamie and Jake were playing quietly together. Playing at pulling down every poster in my room, one by one.

Oh, how I missed my old bedroom, on the second floor of our flat. How I missed the stairgate that stopped the twins from coming in and wrecking my room. How I missed the days when they were tiny babies and couldn't reach doorknobs.

Once I got home, surveyed the damage, had a silent scream to myself and planned ways to kill my brothers, I realized I had to come up with a cunning plan.

And I was staring at it right now, lying flat on my back on the bed. I only hoped those drawing pins were strong enough to keep my posters fixed on to the ceiling. . .

OK, so one problem sorted. Now to try and sort another.

Help – am trapped in Nutsville, I keyed into my mobile, not bothering to sit up. *Please rescue me. Or just talk 2 me! Where r u? luv stella.*

There had never *ever* been a time when me and Frankie had gone for three days without talking, even if it was just by text. We once went for *two* days without talking, when I was on holiday in Greece and something went funny with the mobile reception 'cause of an earthquake. See? It took an earthquake that was 4.5 on the Richter scale to keep us apart. So how come she'd turned silent on me now?

"We'll stay in touch ALL the time, Stella, OK?! Mates for ever, remember!" she'd told me late on Friday night, when Dad came to pick me up from the party. She'd grabbed my arm so tight it practically left a *bruise*. And even though it was dark outside on her doorstep, I was *sure* she had tears in her eyes. Wow – I'd known Frankie since I was three months old (and she was a more mature eight months old), and I'd never *once* seen her cry. You know how couples in movies sometimes say they're each other's other half? Well, it was sort of like that with me and Frankie – I was *her* shy, quiet, bumbling side, and she was *my* fearless, loud, non-crying side. But suddenly everything felt totally muddled. I mean, there she was nearly blubbing on Friday, yet it was Monday night now and if I didn't know her better I'd think she was avoid—

My mobile trilled to life in my hand, jarring my muddled thoughts and nearly making me *lunge* out of my skin.

At last!

"Frankie?" I grinned, sitting bolt upright on the bed as soon as I clocked her number on the illuminated panel of my phone.

"Hi, Stella!"

She sounded fuzzy and far away, further than London, as distant as the dark side of the moon. (She was probably just on the top deck of the 134 bus – you know what mobiles are like.)

"Where've you been? I thought you said you'd get back to me on Sunday! What's been happening?" I laughed, feeling a bit dippy with happiness at hearing her voice.

"Hey, y'know how it is. I was out with the girls and then seeing my gran and stuff and then I ran out of money on my mobie."

"Did you e-mail? 'Cause Dad hasn't set up

the computer here yet so I couldn't pick up any messages," I wittered on, accepting her explanation, even if it *did* have a whiff of lameness about it (hadn't she seen her gran on Saturday?).

"Nah – I didn't get round to it."

I felt a twinge in my stomach that *could* have been indigestion, but since I hadn't eaten anything for a while I kind of suspected it was a twinge of *hurt*.

"Oh. Oh, OK," I shrugged, getting up and walking over to the window, where I pressed my head against the cool glass. Out in the garden, I saw the tail end of my ginger shadow disappear through the one broken pane of the outhouse window. "So . . . how's Neish and everyone?"

"Y'know, same old stuff. How's the new place? Still bleurghhhhh?"

For the last few days I'd been *dying* to tell her all about Portbore and the sheer, drop-dead boringness of it all, but suddenly I didn't feel much like doing that. Maybe it was the way she'd skirted over my question about the other girls just then. I mean, didn't she understand that I still really, *really* needed to feel part of our gang, even if I was just a long-distance member?

"It's all right." I shrugged again. "I'll tell you all

about it when you're here at the weekend."

Uh-oh – there was a sudden, hulking great silence when I mentioned the visit. So it only lasted a split-second, but it was definitely *there*.

"Frankie? You *are* still coming, aren't you?"

"Course!" Frankie laughed. "Got my train ticket already, haven't I?"

Urgh ... I was being paranoid, I was being *so* paranoid. I'd only been here a few days and already Portbore was turning me as mad as half of its inhabitants.

"Friday was brilliant, wasn't it?" I smiled, trying to let go of the paranoia.

"Yeah, it was."

"So ... seen Seb around?"

"Nah."

OK, I'd switched back to being paranoid. What was it with Frankie? How come she was managing to sound so bored? What was with all these nothingy answers, when normally we'd be teasing and joking and chattering away for hours?

"Listen, my mobie's about to pack up – I forgot to charge it," said Frankie. "I'll give you a phone once I'm on the train on Friday, yeah? It's just that my cousin's coming to stay for a few days, so I'll probably be too busy to get in touch till then."

Her cousin Tania? But Tania came for visits all the time, and Frankie wasn't that wild about her, since she was only seven and just wanted to talk about her Bratz dolls all day.

"So speak Friday – OK?" Frankie repeated in a voice that sounded more flat than friendly.

"O-O-O-OK."

It was only once we'd said our very quick byes that I realized something weird about today. When I'd been speaking to that old lady on the beach this morning, I hadn't stammered *once*. But for the first time in my life, I'd stammered talking to Frankie. What was I saying about everything being muddled?

All at once, I wanted to escape, to get out of my stuffy bedroom and be out in the afternoon sunshine in our bee-buzzing, butterfly-bobbing jungle of a garden, where I could breathe in gulpfuls of H_2O and get my head straight. But I didn't want to go back down the stairs, and have Mum and Dad ask me if I was all right, or the twins hurtle themselves at me for a game or a bite or something.

A distant glimmer of ginger through the outhouse window put the idea in my head. I could be out there in the garden, quick as a flash of ginger fur, if I just followed in Peaches' pawprints. . .

Two minutes and some scrambling later and I was knee-deep in wispy grass and elongated dandelions. Staring up at the route I'd just taken from my first-floor bedroom window (out on to the roof of the kitchen, down on to the old wooden coal shed), I couldn't believe what I'd just done. It felt like my blood was swooshing round at high speed, all diluted with adrenaline. It's just that *I* was the girl who was completely rubbish at PE; I mean, seriously, even just last week I got freaked out when Mrs Kitson our PE teacher expected us to jump off the *trampette*. (You should have heard how much teasing I got off Neisha and everyone over *that*. . .)

And all the adrenaline made me bound over a patch of nettles next. Then with one hefty shove of my shoulder against the door, I plunged into the dim, dusty world of the outhouse.

"Puss? I mean, Peaches?" I whispered, waiting for my eyes to adjust after the brightness outside.

"Prrrp!"

And there he was, curled up like an over-stuffed fuzzy cushion on an old desk by the window. At least, he looked like an overstuffed fuzzy cushion compared to the deflated raggedy one he was sprawled on.

The desk and the chair: that was the only furniture I could see in here. The rest of the space was taken up with rusty old gardening tools and a wall full of shelves cluttered with . . . well, *clutter*.

"What's this place, then?" I asked the cat, glancing nervously around for the owners of the many cobwebs I'd just spotted.

"Prrrp!"

With no tarantulas in sight, and feeling a bit daring, I reached out and put a hand on Peaches' tatty fur. His luminous green eyes blinked up lazily at me, as if he was daring me to tell him he needed to use conditioner. (Had someone tried that already? Was *that* why he smelt so good?)

"Hey, I bought you sardines and custard creams! I know you like them!"

Another blink. Very gently, I tried stroking Peaches – I didn't want to shock him and risk that one yellowed fang inserting itself into my hand.

"Prrrrrrrrrrrr. . ."

Phew. He liked it. Or maybe he was just excited about the idea of sardines and custard creams.

"Y'know, this place is grottier than the cottage – just about!" I mumbled to myself and Peaches, as I pulled out a wobbly-looking wooden chair and sat down to survey the cobwebby junk-fest in front of me.

Meanwhile, Peaches made it plain that he didn't care what I was doing, as long as I carried on with the stroking thing. He stretched his short thick legs out into a luxurious stretch, giving me a closer glimpse of the thing he was sitting on. (Boy, that cat liked sitting on things.) It wasn't a saggy cushion after all; it was an old hat, squashed flat. It was made out of brownish, faded felt, and trimmed with ribbons; two flattened, damp-spotted, once honey-coloured ribbons that now trailed down into the desk's one – slightly open – drawer. Peaches' tail flickered above the drawer too, like a hairy third ribbon. Or a furry arrow?

"What's in here, puss?"

I bent over and tugged at the drawer cautiously – in case I disturbed a nest of snoozing mice or something – and found. . .

1) a roll of brittle plain paper, tied with string

2) a roundish piece of wood, with faded blobs of colour on it, like an old-fashioned palette or something

3) an empty ink bottle, and a scratchy-looking old ink pen

4) a knobbly black twig (Huh?)

But then I realized pretty quickly that it wasn't a twig – it was a piece of charcoal, the sort of thing people drew with long ago, before chalk pencils were invented. My heart pitter-pattered again, same as it had when I scrambled down from my bedroom window just now. *This* wasn't just some mouldy brick garden shed.

"D'you think this was a little art studio or something?" I asked Peaches.

Peaches snored in reply, but as I straightened up, I glanced past his torn and tatty ears, and found my eyes settling on a something peeking out from behind a glass jar of bolts on the bottom row of shelves.

It was a wing.

A delicate, watercolour wing.

Stretching out of the chair, my fingers fumbled around in the dust, and pulled out a tiny tarnished frame, and in it, there was a hand-painted fairy, fluttering amongst flowers. It looked ancient. I mean, *seriously* ancient.

"Thought I saw you lurking in here!"

Lungeing out of my skin was turning into a habit today.

"Just doing a bit of exploring?" Dad smiled, a

halo of sunshine ringing his blond hair as he stood in the outhouse doorway.

"Uh-huh," I shrugged, feeling strangely shy, as if I'd been caught snooping around in someone's sock drawer while they'd nipped to the loo.

"Just thought I'd let you know that the computer's up and running. You've got a few messages. Hey, is this the cat that was in your room yesterday?"

Dad had offered to shoo Peaches out of my bedroom last night – back when he was just some strange, stray cat and not Peaches. I was glad now that I hadn't let Dad chase him away – and I'd have to *properly* introduce them to each other and tell Dad what I'd found out about my ginger shadow (i.e. he was weird, he was a wanderer, he liked custard cream biscuits).

But that would have to wait; just like rooting around some more for hidden secrets (and fairies) in the outhouse.

Right now all I wanted to do was brush the decades-old dust off my fingers, get to that computer, and write a great big techno hello to all my mates. . .!

Chapter 8

Frankie and the secret night out

Already the sun was on full beam outside our kitchen window, and it wasn't even 8.30 a.m. yet. It was going to be *baking* hot today.

And already I was feeling the heat – at least my right leg was. Peaches had wrapped himself so much around it that it was like I was wearing a furry moonboot.

"He really likes you, doesn't he?" Mum smiled, peering under the table at Peaches.

She was on the other side of the kitchen table from me and Dad, sitting in between Jake and Jamie's high chairs like a referee, ready to hold up a yellow card next time one of them aimed a soggy Weetabix at the other.

"He likes the bacon on Stella's plate, you mean!" Dad joked.

"So does Stella!" I said, raising my eyebrows and taking another bite of the ketchup-dripping bacon sarnie I'd just made. That was *one* good thing about this move – back home in London it was all healthy cereals for six days of the week, and unhealthy, fattening fry-ups on Sundays only. But this was Tuesday, and for the last four days, all we'd eaten was junk food. It was a bit like being on permanent holiday.

"So he slept on your bed all night again?" Mum asked.

"Mmm," I mumbled and nodded, my mouth full of sarnie.

Yes, Peaches had slept on my bed all night again, and *hadn't* done a disappearing act by the time morning came, even though my window was left open wide enough for him to escape if he'd wanted to.

"Well, if that cat's going to stay here, we'd better get him some *proper* food," said Mum, matter-of-factly. "I don't care what that old lady told you, it's not good for a cat to live on sardines and biscuits."

"And bacon!" Dad chipped in.

I narrowed my eyes and looked at both of them. Were they saying what I *thought* they were saying?

"You mean," I spluttered, gulping my breakfast down too fast, "I can *keep* Peaches?"

"Well, until he gets bored of us, if what that old lady was saying is true!" Dad grinned.

I was sort of in shock. Back in London, I'd tried

everything to get a pet. "Can I get a dog?" "No – its barking would bug the neighbours." "Can I get a cat?" "We don't have a garden – it wouldn't be fair." "Can I have a hamster?" "Their cages get too smelly." "Can I have a goldfish?" "Er, no." (I think my parents had got so used to saying no when it came to pets that it would have felt too weird for them to say *yes*.)

"Er . . . thanks!"

As I mumbled my stunned thank you, I reached down and scratched Peaches' head, and got a pleased "Prrrp!" in reply. Then he got distracted by a milk-mushy Weetabix that had just splatted from on high (courtesy of Jake) and went off to lick that. I think Peaches was going to like it here.

Glancing back up, I caught Mum and Dad giving each other secret little smiles. Hmm . . . what was *that* all about? And after years of being pet-phobic, how come they were suddenly suggesting we adopt this not-particularly-pretty specimen of cat-ness? Unless . . . unless they were just trying cheer me up, or *bribe* me. You know – Stella's not too happy being dragged here to the seaside, so let her keep the fleabag, if it cheers her up?

Not that I needed too much cheering up this morning. I was well chuffed when I checked my e-mails yesterday and found a flurry of hellos from my friends, all written at various times on Saturday – they hadn't forgotten me after all! Well, maybe Neisha had . . . there'd been nothing from her, but to be fair, she didn't have her own computer and during school holidays had to send and get her messages through her mum's computer at work.

". . .the party was great, wasn't it? But ate too much of *everything* and feel sick now, so I thought I'd get up and e-mail you this. Or maybe I just feel sick 'cause I know you're leaving in a few hours! Sniff!" (That was Lauren, at 3.30 a.m. on Saturday.)

". . .Seb is *soooooo* cool. Get butterflies in my tummy when I think of him kissing you! You are *sooooooooo* lucky, Stell!" (Parminder, 9.29 a.m., Saturday.)

"You better stay in touch, Stella Stansfield, or I'll never talk to you again! Ha ha ha!" (Eleni, 11.36 a.m., Saturday.)

". . .me and Mum just finished tidying up the place. Kept finding streamers in weird places – best one was around the INSIDE of the parakeet's cage!" (Frankie, 12.10 p.m., Saturday.)

Aunt Esme wouldn't have been too chuffed about her precious Peetie being meddled with, but then Peetie had a bite worse than Jamie's, so I'd hate to see the hand of the person who'd decorated his cage when no one was looking. . .

"Oh, Stella – I meant to tell you," said Dad suddenly, a lump of scrambled egg speared on his fork. "I checked the computer earlier 'cause I was waiting for a quote back from a company about recycled floorboards."

Because I'm a very polite girl, I resisted the urge to yawn, and waited for Dad to get to the point.

"Anyway, I saw you got an e-mail from Neisha. Sorry, I should have mentioned it earlier. . ."

As I dived from my chair and disentangled my leg from his clutches, Peaches prrrped a surprised prrrp.

"Sorry!" I called back vaguely as I hurried through to pick up the last of my missing messages.

Hi Stella! Soz I didn't get back to your texts – I'm rubbish, I know.

Neisha's e-mail was dated yesterday, Monday, I noticed.

And couldn't sneak into Mum's work and do my e-mails till today. How's the new place? Hope it's not doing your head in. Things OK here – had fun night out on Saturday, but Frankie'll have told you about that already, I guess. We just hung out near the ponds on the Heath. Loads of people there – right laugh. Parminder dared Lauren to stick her feet in the water (you know how the ponds freak Lauren out – you'd think there were sharks in there or something!), and then Seb ran over and picked her up and pretended he was going to chuck her in! Lauren was going mental, but it wasn't like he was seriously going to do it!

Oops – Mum says her boss has just come in so I gotta go.

More soon!

Neish xxx

It took three read-throughs of Neisha's e-mail for me to work out why it bugged me so much. And then – of course – I realized. I'd spoken to Frankie last night, even if it *was* just a weirdly short, weirdly weird call, and she hadn't said *anything* about hanging out with Seb on Saturday night.

What exactly was my so-called best friend playing at?

"Look, I'm *sure* Frankie didn't tell you because she didn't want to rub it in," Mum suggested, expertly shooting out a hand and pulling the plastic tractor from Jamie's hand before he knew it was gone. "Bet you she didn't want you to feel bad about being so far away from your friends and what they were up to!"

"Maybe," I shrugged, leaning over the twin's buggy to inspect the damage Jamie's tractor had inflicted on Jake's nose (it wasn't *too* bad – only a medium-sized, throbbing red thump).

"The thing is, Stella –"

(Mum suddenly had to raise her voice, as Jamie began a mournful where's-my-toy-gone? howl.)

"– I think you're just feeling a little bit, well, *vulnerable* just now. All this –"

(She waved one hand around, as if she was talking about the shops on Portbore's minuscule high street.)

"– is *bound* to be unsettling for you. And Frankie's never let you down before, has she?"

I shook my head, as we passed a butcher's with a gruesome collection of meat slapped in the window.

"Well, then, just give her the benefit of the doubt. You can ask her all about it this weekend.

And – oh! Hey, look at this!"

Back in London, Mum got her hair cut at this flash, West End hairdresser that was part of a chain run by one of those guys who's always on telly ads flogging their straightening serums or whatever. Even after she'd stopped working ('cause of the twins), she still trekked to the same place, and wouldn't have stepped inside the *local* hairdresser's for a zillion pounds. Yet here she was, cooing over *The Style Compony Hair & Beauty Salon*, which looked about as glamorous as the butcher's next door.

"Stella, could you look after the boys for a sec? I just want to nip in and get a price list!"

Before I could say "OK", she'd disappeared inside, leaving me with the Muppets. It wasn't that I minded looking after Jake and Jamie. They couldn't embarrass me with their wailing (I was too used to it), but what *was* embarrassing was my mum's twittery excitement about this crummy place, a business that couldn't even spell its own *name* right. I mean, if the "Style Compony" was dyslexic on its fancy painted sign above the door, how good were they going to be at cutting hair and doing manicures? I'd be terrified I'd go in for highlights and come out with only one eyebrow.

"Anyway," I mumbled, crouching down and talking to Jake, who was happily smiling despite the throbbing bump on his nose, "what's the point of Mum getting a facial and her nails done when we live on a building site?"

"Hammer go BOOOMM!" Jake roared energetically.

Oh, yes, back home at the building site, a hammer was most definitely going boom. Straight after breakfast, Dad had taken a sledgehammer to a defenceless wall. The noise had been so bad that Peaches had vanished on his travels, and I'd had no choice but to come out shopping with Mum and the Muppets.

"Big lorry, big *LORRY*!"

That was Jamie, who'd stopped crying over his lost toy/weapon now that he had something bigger to ogle at. I felt the lorry before I saw it; the ground was trembling with the rumble of it. Or *them*, actually, since a whole convoy of trucks was thundering its way slowly down the high street, heading in the direction of the beach. Vast sheets of tarpaulin were stretched over the oddest of cargoes – vast, multicoloured arcs of metal dotted with rows of bulbs.

All the Fun of the Fair! read a logo on the side

of the first truck, now signalling right, past the fish and chip shop, to turn on to the prom.

And down at the bottom of the road, where the convoy was headed, I could have sworn I saw a flash of ginger fur disappearing behind the distant *Fresh haddock!* sign propped up on the pavement. . .

"Well! They're certainly very friendly in there!" Mum beamed, coming back out on to the sunny pavement clutching a bunch of leaflets.

I nearly jumped when I saw a small, middle-aged woman waving at me through the shop window: a vision of vivid lipstick, blusher and fluffy clouds of bleached blonde hair just 20 centimetres away from me through the glass.

"The owner gave you a lovely compliment!" Mum beamed, taking charge of the buggy and steering us away. "She said you had stunning hair!"

"Yeah, but I bet they wouldn't know how to cut hair like *mine*!" I grumbled, finding it hard to take a compliment from someone with a candyfloss hairdo (all that was missing was the *stick*).

"How do you know they've got no experience with afro hair?" Mum suddenly frowned at me. "You don't like it if people make assumptions about *you*, Stella, so you shouldn't go around making assumptions about other people!"

Urgh. . . I hated getting told off by Mum. It made me feel about as big as the boys. Feeling my face deepen to scarlet, I kept my eyes fixed on the glimpse of the sea just past the traffic lights and stayed schtum. Even the boys seemed to sense that Mum had snapped at me and shut up. Finally, after an agonizing three second silence, Mum spoke first.

"By the way, you know how you were asking about your grandad the other night?"

I shot her a shy sideways glance and nodded.

"Well, I got thinking last night, and I wondered if your nana had kept any letters from him, or souvenirs maybe."

My heart went *thud!* like something heavy had just dropped in my chest.

"The thing is," Mum continued, "I've still got a couple of boxes of her personal things that I cleared from her house when she died. I can't remember anything in particular being *in* there, but then I wasn't in a great mood when I was sorting through it at the time, so maybe I missed something."

"And you've never looked in those boxes in all

these years?!" I almost gasped, wondering how she could *do* that. Wasn't she in the least bit curious? Wasn't she interested in the possibility of finding out more about her own dad? Her own past?

"I didn't think I could face it before. Thought it would make me a bit sad to go through her things."

There I was, making assumptions again. OK, so Mum didn't feel all that strongly about the father she'd never known, but she *was* cut up about the mum she loved and missed. What a goofball I could be.

"If you find anything, that would be cool," I smiled at her. "But it's OK if you don't."

"Good!" Mum smiled back, as pleased as I was to be friends again. "When I get a minute, I'll check through it all."

Ah, now *that* was the problem.

Between getting the house straight, trying to discourage my dad from demolishing the place around our ears, and stopping the twins from hitting, biting or generally torturing each other, the next time Mum was likely to get a spare minute was probably about a *decade* away. . .

Chapter 9

The way to Sugar Bay. . .

I've got two crystal-clear memories from childhood.

One is of Mum yelling, "No! Don't lick *that*!" when I was about three and curious to see what flavour slugs were.

The other is of a day trip to Southend with Aunt Esme and Frankie when me and Frankie were about four. I can't remember much about the day trip itself, but I remember sitting next to Frankie on the train home, comparing treasures we'd found on the beach. Frankie's included a dead starfish, a big stick and a stone in the shape of a bum (sort of). My treasures were two pockets crammed with seashells and a mangy piece of tinfoil that I was convinced was part of a mermaid's tail, and absolutely *wouldn't* let Aunt Esme take it off me and put it in the bin where it belonged.

Well, I don't think I'd have got all that excited by the glitter of a minging sliver of tinfoil these days, but my pockets were rapidly filling up with sheeny-shiny shells. Don't know why I was bothering to collect them though; if I took them home, Jake and Jamie would probably just *eat* them or something.

After this morning's exciting shopping trip (i.e. going to the chemist's, the hairdresser's and the world's smallest branch of Woolworths), Mum, me and the boys had come home for lunch, only to find that Dad had sledgehammered his way through a water pipe in the wall. I thought Mum might pick up the sledgehammer and do some damage to *Dad* with it, but instead, she helped Jake and Jamie into their wellies, handed them some toast, and let them eat their "lunch" on the move, gleefully kicking around in the puddle on our dining-room/disaster-zone floor. Twenty minutes later, the boys were just going down for their nap when the emergency plumber arrived, so I abandoned my mop, got out of the way, and escaped down here to the beach.

At first, I whiled away the time sitting on the sand texting all of my mates. *Bored, hot, miss u guys. What u up 2? Luv stella.* I tried not to think about the fact that this was the fourth time I'd texted Lauren, Eleni and Parminder, and heard exactly *zilch* back from them since their flurry of Saturday e-mails. (I'd forgive Neisha, since she'd e-mailed just yesterday.)

Texting done, I doodled in the sand with my finger and then got into some people-watching. There were loads of families sunbathing (i.e. going various shades of lobster pink); some small kids happily burying another small kid in the sand (and ignoring his pleas to let him up); a bunch of day-tripping OAPs paddling in the shallows (giggling like they were seven and not 70); a short kid walking a big, hairy Alsatian (or maybe it was the other way around); and I even saw the woman from the Style Compony, letting her high heels sink in the sand as she held the leads of two small dogs that looked like the waddling equivalent of the blonde bouffant on her head (she waved, but I pretended I was watching the OAPs and didn't wave back).

After that, I tried lying down and watching the seagulls swirl around in the sky, but it made me kind of dizzy. So I stood up and started strolling, picking up shells that took my fancy, stopping to gawp for a minute at the fairground lorries unloading in the prom car park, and then found myself slap-bang running out of beach. Towering in front of me instead was a big cliffy bit of rock, partly covered in grass, with a meandering path weaving up it. Holding a hand above my eyes, I squinted at the two signs in front of me, at the top of the short flight of concrete steps that led up from what was left of the beach to the start of the path. One of the signs was made out of metal, and in red lettering on a bright-yellow background, it said *Seaview Holiday Homes* (must have taken the caravan park owners all of three seconds to come up with *that* name). The other sign was wooden, badly faded, and hard to read.

"*Uger ay...*" I mumbled to myself, then bounded up the steps – shells clanking together in my pockets – for a better squint.

Sugar Bay.

While my head was still processing that information, my feet had already made up their mind – the faded arrow next to the faded lettering was aimed up the path and over the hill, and that's where my trainers were taking me.

Five breathless minutes later, I was at the top of the headland, staring at a breathtaking view of . . . caravans. Well, OK, it was caravans straight in front of me, but if I turned around and looked back the way I'd come, there was a pretty, er, *pretty* view of the town and the bustling beach below, stretching right along to the bobbing masts of small boats in the faraway harbour.

"Cawww!"

I flipped my head back round at that ugly sound, and saw one of Portbore's huge seagulls surveying me from the roof of one of the caravans.

"'Cawww' to you too!" I called to it, wondering if it was any relation to the fairy-cake fan from yesterday.

In what felt like slow motion, the big bird extended its wings, flopped off the roof and seemed to be aiming itself straight at *me*. I was just about to panic and break the world speed record for Hurtling Back Down A Windy Path when the bird spun lazily round and with a couple of flaps disappeared over the metal roofs, towards . . . well, towards Sugar Bay, as my trainers seemed to know, even if my brain didn't. Stomping my way around a few white, cream and grey caravans, I suddenly stopped dead as the view opened up in front of me.

Sugar Bay curved below like a new moon, the tiny bay as blue as those you see in the Caribbean on holiday programmes on telly. The beach looked like someone (very big) had poured out tonnes of demerara sugar around the edge of the grassy hills that swooped down to meet the water. (Was that how it got its name?) And the weirdest thing about the beach was that it was empty: not an ice-cream van, not a kid, not even a sandcastle was in sight. How come none of the holidaymakers from Seaview was down there? But then maybe the lure of 99 cones, candyfloss and public toilets on Portbore Beach won them over.

Or maybe the house put them off.

The Big House the old lady had told me about yesterday ... there it was, fancy and grand but falling down, like a cross between a wedding cake and the sort of place the Addams Family might live in. I was kind of spooked by the look of it, but luckily – or *unluckily*, depending on your point of view – my feet were much braver, and started walking down the gravelly path towards it.

As I got closer, I could see red brickwork peeking through the decades-old (centuries-old?) cream paintwork. There were gaping holes in the glass windowpanes – windows like a more glam version of the one tiny window in the outhouse I'd been exploring this morning. (Bored thugs must have been using it as target practice. Then again, it was so old, maybe *generations* of bored thugs were responsible for the damage.) As I got closer still, the garden reminded me of our overgrown jungle too – this one was a muddle of daisies, dandelions, tangled rose bushes and towering purple somethings.

I leant on the ornate, rusted fence that ran round the garden and stared up at the crumbly grandness of it, but for the *brave* part of me (i.e. my feet), that wasn't enough. And so I ducked through the gap where a couple of railings had rusted away, pushed my way through the under-growth, passed an ivy-covered sign that read *Dan keep out!* (ignoring the fact that there was almost definitely a "ger" lurking under those ivy leaves) and found myself at a window. Only problem was, my eyes were in line with the *sill*.

In a manoeuvre Mrs Kitson my old PE teacher would have been proud of (hey, I was turning into a bit of a gymnast today, if you counted the scramble from my bedroom to the garden too), I launched myself up, scrabbling my trainers on the brickwork and breathlessly thudded my elbows on to the cold, paint-peeling sill.

And I saw . . . nothing. 'Cause right then, my

mobile started ringing and I started slithering, and landed back on the daisies with a thud, and a crunch of shells in my jeans pockets.

"Hi Stella!"

"Mum?" I panted.

"Why are you breathless? Where are you?"

Clambering around a condemned building didn't sound like the sort of answer she'd be delighted to hear, so I told her . . . the truth. Well, it was the truth, five minutes earlier.

"Just walked up the hill to the caravan park, so I could check the view."

"Really? That's nice!"

Let me translate: Mum had just said, "You're kidding? That's brilliant! I thought you hated this place!"

"So what are you phoning for?" I asked, idly plucking at some of the big purple somethings beside me.

"Er . . . do you remember that old-fashioned ironmonger's we passed this morning?"

"Nope," I told her, staring at the rows of bell-shaped blossoms on the long, straggly stalks in my hand.

"Yes you do – it's on the high street."

"Don't remember it," I said warily, wondering

what this was all about. Mum obviously wanted me to pick up something on the way home (again). But I didn't even know what an ironmonger sold. Iron? Had Dad broken something else that only iron could fix?

"You *do*!" Mum insisted. "It's in between the newsagent and the undertaker!"

I don't know if it was the mention of the undertaker that gave me the shivers, but suddenly, I didn't feel in much of a rush to look inside that dark window above me. Suddenly, my feet felt as cowardly as the rest of me and I started picking my way across the garden.

"So you want me to buy something from there?" I asked, wriggling my way speedily through the gap in the railings, and trailing the flowers behind me like a peacock feather.

"Um, yes please. Some stain remover for ink. They're bound to sell it."

"What's Dad done this time?" I grinned, glancing over my shoulder at the house, now that I was a safe, non-spooky distance away.

"It's not your dad. It's, er, Jamie. He found a felt pen somewhere and started drawing. On your duvet cover. Sorry."

You know, I didn't care if they were only two

years old and didn't know any better – Jamie and Jake were going to *have* to stay out of my room, if they wanted to make it to *three*. . .

Chapter 10

Broken shells and cheery "bleep!"s

"Could I have a fuse, please?"

"Certainly," the mild-mannered bald man behind the counter smiled at the woman in front of me. "What size? Three amp, five amp, 13 amp?"

"Er, is there a difference?" the woman asked, sounding flummoxed.

"Well, yes, if you don't want to fit the wrong size to your appliance and burn your house down."

Good grief, this woman sounded as useless at DIY as my dad. But I didn't mind that there was a dithery customer ahead of me in the ironmonger's – it gave me a chance to practise asking what I wanted in my head, in the hope that I wouldn't curl up with shyness and start stammering. (I'm a big fan of supermarkets and mini-markets – you pick what you want and hand over the money, no talking or stammering required.)

It also gave me a chance to gawp around the shop – now that I was here, it looked like the sort of place that might sell huge, toddler-repelling padlocks for bedroom doors. I didn't have enough money on me to get one today, but I'd know where to come back to. . .

"Foxgloves!"

"Huh?"

My mind had been too full of the joy of padlocks to notice that Mrs Fuse had been dealt with and that the baldy bloke behind the counter was ready to help me out. Except I didn't know what he was on about.

"Foxgloves!" he smiled some more, pointing to the long, lanky purple flowers I'd taken with me from the garden of the house in Sugar Bay.

"Oh! That's the name of our house!" I squeaked in surprise at the coincidence.

"Foxglove Cottage? Very nice place – needs a bit of work though!"

I could see a happy twinkle in the shopkeeper's eye, as if he could sense months' worth of custom coming his way now a family of mugs from London had moved into the old, falling-down shack.

"Uh-huh," I nodded, wondering if the lake on the ground floor had been fixed by now – I'd forgotten to ask Mum when she'd called. "Have you got any stain remover, for ink, please?"

I suddenly felt quite proud of myself: I'd been so taken aback to find out what a foxglove looked like and then got caught up in fleeting visions of wearing wellies to breakfast in the morning that I'd forgotten to be nervous in front of this stranger.

"Stain remover? For *ink*? Are you sure that's the one you want?"

"Uh, yes, please," I told him, instantly feeling as flummoxed as Mrs Fuse. What was this guy on about?

"Oh, right. It's just that I thought you were after something to remove *that*."

Omigod, he was pointing at my *chest*!

"Red-brick dust is a devil to get out!" he blustered, suddenly looking excruciatingly shy himself, as if he'd realized the boob (argh!) he'd made. "Like the . . . um . . . like the stamens on lilies! Terrible, they are. . ."

We were *both* blushing now. And then it dawned on me what he was trying to get across. I glanced down and saw that the front of my pale pink T-shirt was covered in vivid, gingery-red powder.

"So, er, been up to Josephs' House, then?" he asked, pulling a box packed with stain removers off a shelf and rifling through it. "Only place around

106

here built of red brick. They imported it specially when they were building the place! Of course they went and painted it when the fashion changed."

Luckily, he was rifling so hard in the box that it gave me precious seconds to figure out what he meant *now*.

"The house in Sugar Bay?" I checked with him. "Is that what it's called?"

"Oh, yes. Magnificent, it must have been, in the old days," the man chattered away, looking relieved to be off the uncomfortable subject of my chest. "Time's running out for it now, of course. It's getting demolished at the end of summer, to make way for luxury holiday chalets."

Can you feel sad for a house? If you'd asked me before, I'd have said I didn't think so, but now there was a tug at my heart at the thought of that grand old place being torn down and carted away in dumper trucks. It was the same sort of painful tug I felt when I thought of dirty, overcrowded, wonderful London and the brilliant friends I'd had to leave behind. ...

But a small "bleep!" soon cheered me up. I heard it just as I stepped out of the ironmonger's shop and on to the sun-bleached pavement, holding the foxgloves in the crook of one arm while I stuffed the stain remover into the front pocket of my jeans, which were already stuffed with (broken?) shells.

From my back pocket, I grabbed my phone, gagging to see who'd texted me.

You have 1 new message.

Top of my wish list would have been a message from Seb, saying *hi, how are you?* (I *wish!*), and bottom would have been Mum texting to tell me the boys had set my room on fire or something. But anything in between – *any* contact with the outside world – would be *bliss*.

Know something u need to know – can't talk now will call u later. N xxx

Neish! It was from Neisha!

Now it was my stomach's turn to do gymnastics; flipping into a few forward rolls and doing a star jump with excitement. Maybe it was some weird psychic thing, but with a sudden rush I knew, KNEW, KNEW that the "something" I needed to know about was connected with Seb. Had he been asking about me? I didn't know whether I felt more like singing or being sick with sheer happiness.

One thing was for sure – I'd be counting the *seconds* till Neisha phoned me. . .

Chapter 11

A watched mobile never rings

Fourteen thousand, four hundred and twenty seconds later, and I was *still* waiting for Neisha to call.

"Stella! Careful!" Mum frowned at me, as she tried to prise Bob the Builder's sponge head out from between Jamie's four front teeth.

Oops. Guess I *had* been rubbing Jake's grubby face with the flannel a little bit too long; I'd probably taken a layer of skin off as well as the different shades of dirt he had smeared on it.

"Sorry," I mumbled, dropping the flannel in the water and staring at my brother's face for signs of grazing or scuffing. But Jake was fine. He just said "Boo!" and then blew spit bubbles out of his chubby, baby lips at me. (Yuck.)

To tell the truth, I hadn't been concentrating much on the twins' bathtime – after doing my mental arithmetic to figure out how long it had been since I'd heard from Neisha, I'd gone on to wonder how many seconds it had been since I'd heard from Eleni, Lauren and Parminder. I'm not very good at doing maths in my head and after a few attempts, I'd settled on twelvety trillion before Mum hauled me up about accidentally smothering Jake with the facecloth.

Then I heard the sound I'd been waiting for. . .

"Can I. . .?" I started, turning to Mum with a hopeful expression at the sound of the phone ringing.

Walking home from the ironmonger's; helping Mum wash and hang out my duvet cover; all through tea . . . I'd kept staring at my mobile, willing it to trill into life. And when I wasn't doing all *that* stuff, I was running through to the cupboard my dad was optimistically calling his "office" and checking the computer in case Neisha had decided to spill her news by e-mail. There'd been nothing. But maybe this was Neish now, calling on the house phone!

"Let your dad get it – the boys, remember?"

The boys. . . How could I forget? It took two of us (i.e. a rotating combination of Mum, Dad and me) to look after them when they were in the bath. That's 'cause something pretty bizarre happened whenever they came in contact with water: it was like they mutated into hyperactive octopuses, capable of chucking *more* toys and inflicting *more* damage on fixtures, fittings and each other than when they were on dry land (which is saying something).

Actually, it was probably Dad's turn to let one of us off the hook with bathtime duties, but our routine had kind of gone out the window – along with our normal lives – since we'd arrived. And last time I saw him, Dad was headed out to the skip with a dripping roll of soggy lino balanced on his shoulder.

I bit my lip, but did as I was told, turning my attention back to Jake and his spit bubbles while I waited to hear Dad answer the phone . . . and then – hopefully – call for me to come and get it?

"Andy?" Mum shouted, as the phone kept ringing.

"ANNNDEEEEE!" Jamie mimicked her, for the sheer fun of having something to yell.

"He must be still out at the skip," I told her, when we heard nothing but silence in reply. My heart was thudding in my chest – I was desperate not to let that caller slip away unanswered.

"The answerphone will click on," Mum said assuredly, standing Jamie up and getting ready to lift him out of the bath.

"ANSRAPHONNNNNE!!" Jamie threw his head back and bellowed.

"Mum, Dad hasn't set up the answerphone machine yet, remember?"

Mum looked at my imploring face and gave in. "OK, go get it!" she half-smiled, half-shrugged.

I was out like a shot, Jamie's roars of, "GO GET ITTTTTT!!" ringing in my ears.

"Hello?" I panted, after jumping down the rickety stairs five steps at a time.

"Hello! How's my favourite niece?"

Auntie V – great. The only gossip I was likely to hear from *her* was the ridiculous demands of her latest client (there was always some actor wanting flowers/pizzas/Toblerone in their dressing rooms written into their contract). But that wasn't the type of gossip I was interested in tonight.

"Auntie V, I'm your *only* niece," I pointed out, spotting a non-compliment when I heard one.

"Favourite niece, only niece – what's the difference?" she said breezily. "So anyway, how are you enjoying life in your new hovel?"

I couldn't help grinning at Auntie V's cheerful sarkiness.

"The hovel is horrible," I smiled. "It's damp. And smelly. And there's black mould on the bathroom wall, and the bottom of the toilet's all green for some reason."

"Yee-*eewww*," Auntie V grimaced from the comfort of her posh flat in Highgate, with its tasteful antiques and framed theatre posters on the walls.

"Yeah," I added, warming to my theme, "and some plaster fell off the kitchen ceiling tonight, straight into the risotto Dad was making!"

"Oh, that's *gross*, Stella! What did you do, did you have to send out for something to eat?"

"There's only a fish and chip shop here, and they don't deliver!" I laughed, thinking how much Auntie V would loathe Portbore, since it didn't have any of her essentials for life (Chinese takeaways, heaps of theatres, antique markets, posh coffee shops that sold drinks called frappamochachino or whatever).

"How depressing!" Auntie V sighed theatrically. "And what's Portbay like, then?"

"It's Port*bore*, and it's a dump," I set her straight, sort of enjoying being as sarcastic as *she* was for once. It was quite a buzz feeling like I was bantering along with Auntie V, instead of her being my glamorous, confident, mouthy aunt and me being just shy and quiet Stella the non-star. . .

"Poor darling . . . you must really be missing Frankie etc."

I knew Auntie V said "etc." to save time, but it also saved her from remembering details she couldn't be bothered to remember – like the names of all my other friends.

"Yeah, I am. But Frankie's coming at the weekend."

"And so am I!"

"You are?" I gasped, thrilled at the idea of having two allies in the house at the same time.

"Oh, yes – I'm coming to see the slum for myself. But I'm only there on Sunday, for the day – I told your dad that he can't expect me to stay overnight till the place is habitable!"

"Well, you'll never stay, then!" I giggled. "The house was a disaster to start with, but he's making it worse – he flooded the place this morning!"

"Oh, God . . . don't tell me any more, Stella, or I'll change my mind about coming, even for just the day!" Auntie V groaned. "Anyway, is Mr DIY Disaster around? I'd better have a quick word. . ."

"Sure, I'll go and find him," I told her, still smiling.

"No need to find me; I'm here," Dad said softly, from somewhere close by.

You know Aunt Esme's catchphrases? Well, growing up, me and Frankie had one favourite: "Don't do bad things – bad things have a habit of coming back and biting you on the bottom!" We loved it 'cause it sounded so silly, not to mention good and rude (to us six year olds anyway). But *finally* I think I saw the point of that particular saying. After mouthing off so sarcastically to Auntie V, turning around and clocking the look of hurt and disappointment on Dad's kind face made me feel *terrible*.

Yep, I think I'd done a bad thing and just had it come back and bite me on the bottom. . .

Where are u? What's the thing I need to know? Luv S, I tippety-tapped into my phone.

After I'd zapped that text off to Neisha, I bit my lip and stared out of my bedroom window, watching – but not really seeing – the seagulls swirling in the streaky pink, sunset-tinged sky.

I was freaked out, if you want to know the truth. OK, so I'd spoken to Frankie once and had an e-mail and a (mysterious) text off Neisha, but none of my other friends had got back to any texts or messages I'd left on their mobiles the last few days. Er . . . had they *all* forgotten to charge them, or swipe their top-up cards lately? With my heart sinking faster than the *Titanic*, I wondered if – when it came to my gang of girls back in London – little old faraway me was out-of-sight and out-of-mind.

Then I realized – doh! – that I was being paranoid again. This was starting to be a habit, I frowned to myself. All I needed to do to put my angsty mind at rest was call them on their home numbers, instead of their switched-off mobiles.

I was just about to start with Neisha (since she was the one with the hot gossip), when there was a light knock at my bedroom door.

"Come in," I called out wobbly-voiced, feeling myself tense in case it was Dad. I still felt kind of sick at how upset he looked when he caught me whingeing to Auntie V an hour or so ago.

"Hey. . .!"

Urgh, it *was* Dad. Just chuck a bucket of guilt over me right now.

"Come and see this, Stella!" he beckoned me.

He seemed OK – not as gutted as he'd looked earlier. I slid off the bed and followed him out of my room, wondering what he wanted to show me, and wondering if I could manage to say sorry to him without a) feeling horribly embarrassed, and b) stammering.

"Check this out!" Dad said softly, opening the door to the twins' room and treading quietly inside, which was actually kind of hard to do considering every floorboard in our house creaked like a cross between a mouse squeak and a loud fart every time you hovered a foot over one of them.

"Aww. . ."

Awkward as I felt around Dad right that second, I couldn't help smiling at my brothers, all tucked up in the cots they were rapidly outgrowing. It's corny to say it, but little kids do look angelic when they're asleep. Well, maybe Jake and Jamie didn't look *angelic* exactly – Jake had a fat finger wedged comfortably up one nostril and Jamie had drool all down his chin – but it *was* very cute, the way they'd stuck their arms through the bars and snoozed off holding hands. . .

"They haven't got a lot to worry about, have they?" Dad suddenly surprised me by murmuring affectionately, wrapping one of his arms around my shoulders and squeezing tight.

I didn't know what Dad meant exactly. And, anyway, I was pretty sure that Jake and Jamie did their fair share of toddler-sized worrying (Jamie: "Is that fat kid going to steal my fish finger again?"; Jake: "Is that skinny kid going to bite me again?").

"What I'm trying to say is, I know it's going to take you a while to settle in here, Stella, and I totally understand that it's not an easy thing to do," Dad carried on, as we both stared down at the snoozling, drooling boys. "But remember it's hard for your mum and me too; once we've got the house straight, I'm going to have to find a new job, and it's not easy for your mum to leave all her friends and London behind. . ."

I suspected that Dad was trying to comfort me. But all it did was confuse me even *more*.

"So, we've all got to give it a bit of time, yeah, Stell?"

Suddenly, I felt kind of *mad* at him for making out that me, him and Mum were all in the same boat, 'cause that wasn't exactly true, was it? After all, *they* chose to move here – *I* didn't.

OK, so now I was simultaneously confused

and mad, and the clash of those two feelings made me plain *nervous*. And what do I do when I'm nervous? Well, I clam up; usually after a tongue-tied stammer or two.

"Um, O-O-O-OK, D-Dad. . ." I mumbled in vague reply, ducking slightly to get out from under his arm before zooming out of the room so fast that the floorboards didn't even have time to squeak/fart. . .

Chapter 12

Peace and toast

"Huurrrrunggg-uuurrr-uurr-uurr. . .!"

It was quarter to eight, it was Wednesday morning, it was two days till Frankie arrived, and the loudest snorty snore in the world – snored about two centimetres from my ear – had just woken me up.

"Morning, Peaches," I blinked sleepily at the scruffy lump of cat sprawled across my pillow in a dappled shaft of sunlight. "Where've you been?"

I hadn't seen him since yesterday morning, when Dad had begun demolishing walls and water pipes with the sledgehammer.

"Humph-urr-urr. . ." Peaches snored in reply, his chunky hairy legs and uneven whiskers twitching as he chased a seagull or a sardine in his dreams.

Y'know, last night I'd really hoped he'd come hopping in through my window: I could have done with the company (or at least a friendly, furry cuddle), since I was feeling a bit, well, *weird* after that odd, one-sided talk with Dad in the boys' room. But sadly, the only thing that had come through the open window was a breeze that smelled of salt, seaweed and peaches and cream. When I finally fell asleep, my dreams were full of me running along sand-covered corridors in strange, old, crumbly houses, never finding the way out, or the way home. . .

"Hey!" I muttered softly, pushing myself up on my elbow for a closer inspection of a strange something dangling around Peaches' neck. "That's a bit of a girly collar for you!"

Not that it was a collar exactly; more a chain, a soft-petalled daisy chain. Who'd put *that* around his neck? Some little girl trying to give this scruffbucket a makeover?

"Stella, are you awake?" I heard Mum's voice drift from the other side of my bedroom door.

"Uh-huh!" I mumbled. She must have heard me muttering to Peaches.

"A-ha! I see the wanderer has returned!" Mum smiled, sticking her head around the door and nodding at my fat cat.

"Um, yeah," I nodded, wondering if she and Dad had talked about me last night, after I'd practically walked out on Dad in mid-conversation and hid out in my room for the rest of the night. But nothing in Mum's normal, friendly face gave anything away.

"Listen," she said, tucking a chunk of dark hair behind her ear, "a postcard's just arrived for you!"

"Who from?" I frowned, even though I felt a flutter of excitement.

"Well, you'll just have to come downstairs and see, won't you?" Mum teased. "It's on the kitchen table. If you get dressed first, I'll have a fried egg and toast waiting beside it! Oh, and cat food for your friend, of course!"

Two minutes, clean underwear, my Bugs Bunny T-shirt and denim mini later, I was padding down the stairs (wishing I'd slipped on my flip-flops, to avoid that common condition in these parts: splinters-of-the-toes). Peaches hadn't even stirred when I'd whispered "Tuna Felix!" in his ear, so I'd left him happily sprawled on my pillow.

At the bottom of the stairs I hesitated, almost turning to the computer cupboard on automatic pilot to check my e-mails (if our computer was a human, I think it would have accused me of *stalking* it). But I resisted, lured by the wonderful waft of Sunday-breakfast-on-a-Wednesday and *more* than curious to see who the postcard was from, even though I suspected it was only some *Greetings From Cromer!* silliness from Grandpa and Granny in Norfolk.

"Hi, honey!" Dad beamed at me, as he heaped a mound of scrambled egg on Mum's plate. "One slice of bacon or two?"

Looked like he didn't realize how weirded out I'd felt when we spoke last night – or he was just pretending, at least. Either way, it was fine by me – I just wanted to forget it too.

"Two, please," I smiled shyly, slithering into the nearest chair.

Mum had put the foxgloves in her favourite tall glass vase in the middle of the table, I noticed. Still, the size they were, I couldn't *miss* them, really.

Speaking of missing. . .

"Where're Jake and Jamie?"

"Not awake yet, for once. Great, isn't it?" Mum grinned, looking like she was really going to enjoy eating a mountain of breakfast using a knife and fork, instead of snatching the occasional bite of toast in between feeding, wiping and restraining the twins. "Anyway, there's your card!"

The front of the postcard Mum had just flipped

across the table towards me showed a head-and-shoulders picture of the Queen, complete with round specs, crossed eyes and a moustache hand-drawn on in blue pen.

"Frankie!" I grinned, spotting her handiwork straight away. And sure enough. . .

Big hi from London! Can't WAIT till Friday. The Kentish Town girls versus Portbay – hurray! Frankie xxx

"That's sweet of her, isn't it?" said Mum, meaning – I guess – that it was sweet of Frankie to send me a postcard, not sweet of her to go defacing Prince William's granny.

"Yeah, it is," I smiled, forgiving Frankie instantly for being so rubbish at keeping in touch since I left London. After all, what were a few lame days compared to a lifetime of being a top friend?

"Um, Stella, while we've got a bit of peace, your mum and I wanted a quick word with you," said Dad, plonking a plate of egg, bacon and beans in front of me, even though I'd instantly lost my appetite for them 'cause of what he just said.

Uh-oh . . . what was coming? Was I about to get a lecture about my attitude?

"Stella, like your dad was trying to say last night, we know this move has been hardest on you," Mum began. "And there's not a lot we can do to help make you feel at home here – that'll just happen when it happens."

Y'know, I could feel a stammer tripping about my tongue already and I hadn't even planned on *saying* anything.

"But maybe there is one thing we can do. . ." Dad added, intriguingly. "We know it's annoying for you, now that the boys are finding it easier to get into your room. So yesterday, I was rooting around in the outhouse, and I found these. . ."

Er, I didn't know what exactly I was looking at (or supposed to think exactly). I guess Dad could tell, probably because I wasn't saying anything and was looking as confused as I usually did when my German teacher expected me to understand the dative case.

"They're antique sliding bolts," Mum explained, making sort-of-sense of the two matching, ornate bits of dirty-looking metal in front of me. "They're made of brass; they'll polish up beautifully."

Nope, I still hadn't a clue *what* my parents were on about.

"We're sending all the doors away to be dipped

and stripped soon, Stella," Dad started up again, "and once they're back, I'm going to fit these sliding bolts on either side of your bedroom door – high up – so you can always keep the boys at bay."

As it sank in, I began to smile. They appreciated the fact that I needed my privacy! I'd have been tempted right then and there to give both my parents a hug for being so kind and thoughtful – if they hadn't been responsible for making me move away from London in the first place.

"Tell her the other thing, Andy!" Mum suddenly butted in.

"Ah, yes! Right – we were thinking, till that's done, you could probably do with your own space, for all your art stuff and your bits and pieces."

"So we thought of the outhouse in the garden!"

I blinked at Mum and Dad and then back again. From the smiles on their faces, I think they assumed I was stunned with surprise. Instead I was thinking: "What – you expect me to sit in there, with a bunch of spiders and the dust-mites for company?"

Suddenly I knew what Cinderella felt like. . .

"We can chuck all the rubbish in the skip, and it closes with a hook and eye latch that's too high for Jake or Jamie to reach," Dad chattered away enthusiastically. "And there's even electricity – I fitted a new bulb in the casing and it works fine!"

"And we can clear it out, give it a good going over with a brush and Mr Sheen!" Mum suggested.

Hmm. . . OK, so suddenly I *wasn't* feeling so much like a second-best Cinderella. Maybe having the outhouse as a den could be kind of cool. After all, it had been someone's art studio once, so maybe it could be mine? I could stash my art stuff on the shelves and stick my caricatures around the walls and –

"MEEEEE-*YYYYOWWWWWWW*!" came a cat-in-trouble screech from upstairs.

In the split-second that Mum, Dad and me stared at each other, we heard another terrible, terrifying sound coming from the floor above.

"Hee-hee-hee!"

Uh-oh – twins on the rampage. . .

Chapter 13

Pocahontas of Portbore

I'd found buried treasure.

It was only buried under layers of dust and cobwebs, but it was still treasure. My haul included: a knobbly bottle with the words "ginger beer" on it in raised glass bumps; a rusted box of half-used watercolour paints; a silver-framed mirror with more dark spots on it than actual *mirror*; a pretty, chipped cup with roses painted on it, some old-fashioned decorated tins advertising stuff like sweets and tea (but which had held nails and screws that I'd chucked away), and a small wooden box with the initials *E G* neatly carved on the top (empty, except for a discoloured gold-ish metal button, which I'd kept).

They were now all on display on my newly scrubbed shelves, along with all my art stuff, a framed picture of Grandpa and Granny Stansfield (taken at Christmas last year, with silly paper hats on their heads) and another one of Nana Jones (taken in the late '60s, with lots of make-up and very hairsprayed strawberry blonde hair).

"Hey, it's looking great in here!" said Mum, appearing in the doorway of the outhouse, one hand on the hip of her jeans. The other hand was holding a jam-jar crammed with pastel-coloured sweetpeas and curly, ferny leaves that she must have picked from amongst the weeds in the garden.

"Yeah, it's all right," I agreed, glancing around at the results of five and a half hours' worth of de-scuzzing the place and feeling pretty chuffed with myself – and Dad, of course. Ignoring proper work in the house, he'd helped me out the whole time, making dozens of trips back and forth to the skip with rusted, mangled gardening tools and assorted useless junk. I'd done all the sifting, sorting, discovering of buried treasure and frantic scrubbing – while Mum kept up a steady supply of buckets of hot, soapy water in the few snatched minutes here and there when she managed to escape the twins.

"That's brilliant!" she laughed, plonking the jar of flowers down on the wooden desk by the window, right beside my carefully placed collection of (the unbroken) shells from the beach. She was pointing at the caricature of the old lady I'd met on Monday. I'd pinned it to the corkboard I'd taken down from my room, right next to my drawing of Neisha and Lauren. Also on the board was the photo-booth strip of me and Frankie, the postcard of the cross-eyed Queen and the flyer for the funfair I'd found in my room the other night, under Peaches' fat tummy. There was also a small space for a Polaroid, or *part* of a Polaroid, if I ever (fingers crossed) happened to find the mangled photo of me and Seb.

"It's just all so . . . *cosy!*" Mum smiled, her fingers stroking the smooth surfaces of the shells, while her eyes darted from the felt hat that I'd dusted off and dangled on a nail on the wall, to the tiny fairy painting hanging pride of place beside the window, right above the desk.

"The rug helps. So does the curtain," I told her, feeling grateful for Mum's donations. The multicoloured rug used to live on Dad's office floor in the old flat ("We'll get a new one once his office here is done up," she'd told me), and the "curtain" was a floaty, chiffon sarong of hers ("Don't think it would fit round my bottom since I've had the boys!").

Then I saw her eyes settle on the circle of ginger

furriness balled up and snoring on the armchair that used to be in her and Dad's bedroom back in Kentish Town ("Our room's smaller here – there's not a lot of room for this chair so you might as well have it for your den.").

"Hmm. . ." she muttered, raising an eyebrow. "Seems like Peaches thinks this place is pretty cosy too!"

Peaches did look very rela*aaaaxxxxeeeeddd* indeed – unlike this morning, when we'd caught Jake and Jamie trying to dress him up in one of their toy's clothes. Or maybe he'd just made a meowling fuss because he wasn't a big Fireman Sam fan and didn't particularly want to wear his helmet.

"Hey. . ." I suddenly began, narrowing my eyes and peering at the fat cat. "What's he got there?"

As Peaches snoozed, I noticed that he was tenderly holding something between his two front paws. It was like he was doing an impression of the boys when they were tucked up in their cots, hugging their Boohbahs close to their chests.

"It's a feather, isn't it?" Mum suggested, peering closer herself. "A seagull feather, by the look of it. Hope he didn't kill one to get it!"

"I doubt it," I laughed, wrinkling up my nose.

"Have you seen the size of the seagulls here? They're bigger than *him*!"

"I suppose!" she smiled. "Anyway, never mind seagulls; have you seen *yourself* recently?"

Stepping sideways, I peered into the splotchy mirror I'd hung up on the back wall and checked out my reflection. Eyes, nose, mouth, hair (held at bay in two short, stubby braids); all of them were where they were supposed to be. But my freckles; they were practically hidden under a dark smudge of dirt smeared *right* across my nose and cheeks.

The stripe of dirt put a dumb idea into my head – reaching down, I teased the feather out of Peaches' paws, stuck it in my hair and turned to Mum.

"Am I a dead ringer for Pocahontas, then?" I grinned at her. "What do you reckon?"

"I reckon I should get the camera!" Dad's bright and sea-breezy voice replied instead. "And speaking of photos, is this yours?"

Standing behind Mum in the outhouse doorway, my grinning Dad looked as dirty and dusty as I did. He leant forward and held out a well-crumpled, jaggedly torn photo that looked tiny next to the big red builder's glove he was wearing.

Seb!

"I just looked in on the boys on the way back from the skip," Dad chattered on, "and I caught them posting cornflakes – and this – down the gaps between the floorboards!"

I grabbed the remains of the Polaroid, my heart thundering under my dust-covered T-shirt.

And there was Seb . . . missing.

All I was staring at was my own face gazing back at me, and a big, ripped space where Seb's should have been. . .

Hi Seb, I typed into the keypad, *it's Stella*.

I sat back on the swivel chair and swivelled a bit, trying to figure out what to write next. I'd got the idea to text Seb when I was in the shower, washing plaster dust – and seagull feathers – out of my hair. As the water hammered down, a thought had drummed into my head: *Just text him! Just say hi! What's the worst that can happen? He doesn't text back, that's all. And best that can happen is that he* does *text back. . .!*

So, in a clean T-shirt and denim shorts, I'd sat down at the computer, checked for new mail (none), and began to text. That was twenty minutes ago and I hadn't got any further than, *it's Stella*, something I actually got stuck on quite a lot.

"It's Stella": that's what Frankie always stepped in and said any time anyone ever asked me my name. Usually people looked at us kind of confused, like they were wondering what the deal was with the ventriloquist act. Whatever anybody else thought, I was always totally grateful to Frankie for saving me the embarrassment of stammering, and giving me a few vital seconds to get over my nerves and talk like a normal person.

But with texts and e-mails, I could be brave. For texts and e-mails I didn't need Frankie. Uh, except I *did*, since I didn't know Seb's mobile number. And if there was *one* person who could wangle that information for me, it was Frankie. . .

Hey, Frankie!

How's things? Is your cousin Tania still at yours? Is she still driving you mad? You can moan to me about her on Friday, when you'll be HERE!!!

Anyway, know you're busy, but just a quickie to ask a big – as in *BIG* – favour. Decided to be brave (like you'd be!) and text Seb! Only trouble is, I don't have his phone no. – so if you see him around, can you ask him for it? DON'T tell him it's for me, though (WAY too embarrassing)!

If you could you would be the BESTEST of BEST MATES, which of course you are already!

See you Friday!

stella

PS Neisha texted to say she had some news – then never got back to me to tell me what it was! Got any idea what she's on about? I'm dying to know!

I pressed the paper aeroplane icon on my computer and watched my e-mail to Frankie ping into cyberspace . . . and then felt restless and not sure what to do with myself. So I did what I *usually* did when I was stuck on stuff like homework research, and started flipping around on my favourite sites on the web. First up, I noseyed at a couple of animation sites I liked: one Japanese (Hello Kitty, Neopets, the movie *Spirited Away* – I'm a mug for all things Japanese and cartoony), and one for a mad site with so-bad-it's-good animation of kittens playing in bands.

As usual, it was fun for a while, but the restlessness I was feeling just wouldn't go away, and I found myself staring at a site engine query box and wondering what I should type in next. Then my reflection in the computer screen put an idea in my head; with the sun streaming in behind me, the silhouette of my newly washed, newly springy, light curls looked dark, just like my grandfather's hair must have been. OK, so I couldn't exactly type in "Missing-grandfather-called-Eddie", but at least I could type in *one* detail I knew about his life – where his family came from before they moved to London. I typed in "Barbados".

If those twenty minutes wondering what to text to Seb had dragged, the next hour flew past quicker than a mad gull aiming for a fairy cake. At school, we'd learnt plenty of stuff about the West Indies, and about the horrible slave trade that sent people from Africa to work on the sugar plantations there (especially to Barbados), and all about the *Windrush* and other ships that had brought lots of black West Indians to Britain to live in the 1950s.

All of that had been really interesting, but I'd never thought before about how much it had to do with my missing grandfather, which was basically *everything.* I flicked from one site to another, finding out loads of amazing, fascinating and sometimes kind of *shocking* facts. For example, centuries ago, white officials had these really bizarre, ugly terms for dual heritage children – if I'd lived in those days, I'd have been called a "quadroon", because of my one black grandparent. I mean, "quadroon": it sounds like a mouldy old biscuit made of marzipan or something, doesn't it?

When I thought about it for a sec, it was like I'd been doing non-stop double history lessons all day, starting with hands-on archaeology in the outhouse earlier, and now a chunk of social history on the computer.

Bling!

My fingers hovered in mid-air over the keyboard when I heard the e-mail alert. Frankie – she'd got back to me already!

With a stupid grin splatted across my face, I clicked open her message, and instantly felt the grin melt away.

Hi Stella,
Soz – don't know how to get Seb's number.
Busy with stuff – speak l8r (Friday).

Huh. . .? That was more like *a text* than an e-mail. It was so short and not-very-sweet that I knew something was wrong: was Frankie annoyed with me for asking for her help with the Seb thing? I mean, yeah, it might be mortifying for someone useless like *me* to find out his mobile number, but Frankie was *fearless*. She got a real kick out of charming people and teasing info out of them before they knew what they were saying or doing. What was up with her? How come she could hang out with Seb on Saturday (and not tell me) but suddenly come over too shy to ask him this? And if she didn't want to do it, why didn't she tell me in her usual jokey way? Why hadn't she even bothered to type her name? Where was the smiley we always, *always* put at the bottom of our e-mails to each other?

Up till a moment ago, I'd had my first *almost* good day in Portbore, but now everything had changed; I could sense the black cloud of homesickness and gloom hovering above my head.

"Stella! Tea's ready!" Mum's voice drifted through from the kitchen.

"C-c-c-coming!" I called back, feeling suddenly as queasy as if I was bobbing on a lilo in the middle of a stormy sea. . .

Chapter 14

Chinese whispers in my head

Isn't it funny how boring things can become totally fascinating when you're trying to avoid doing something?

Stuff like cleaning fluff out from under your bed, playing "Boo!" with your kid brothers for two hours solid, checking for split ends . . . all completely snoresville till it's a choice between *that* and *homework*. Then suddenly, it's as if fluff is fascinating, your snot-nosed baby brothers are utterly adorable, and hunting for split ends is the most fun a girl can have.

One day when I was trying to avoid doing my French homework (*quelle barbant!*), I ended up becoming totally fascinated by some dumb telly show talking about that spooky sensation you get where you just *know* someone's watching you. What they were saying was that it's not spooky at all – it's actually pure science. I can't remember exactly *how* the science bit works ('cause, *duh*, I was meant to be doing my French homework), but it's something to do with electrical impulses, the same electrical impulses that help birds fly without bumping into planes or pylons or each other.

Well, I didn't need an electric impulse to let me know I was being stared at right now . . . I could see those two liquid green eyes fixed straight on me like laser beams every time I glanced up from my drawing pad.

"You're putting me off!" I mumbled at Peaches, who was curled up on his armchair in the corner of the outhouse.

He just yawned, one yellow fang glinting, and carried on staring. It was as if he knew (by reading my thoughts or by electrical impulse, maybe) that I was trying to do a caricature of him, which was making him look a bit like a furry sack of potatoes with a face.

"OK, fine!" I shrugged, tearing up my unfinished effort and starting again. "Anyway, you don't deserve a picture, not after what *you* did."

Peaches blinked blankly, completely unfazed by the scrunching of the paper or my hopeless efforts at telling him off. But I *had* been grumpy with him this morning, when I woke up (thanks to him snoring) and found dusty red pawprints catwalked right across my newly washed and de-inked white duvet cover. So much for what the baldy bloke in the ironmonger's was saying about the Josephs' house being the only place in the area built of red brick – Peaches had definitely scampered around somewhere built of the same stuff. I mean, even though I'd seen him sunbathing as far as the beach, there's no *way* he could wander as far as Sugar Bay. Could he?

Could he. . .?

I was back at the Josephs' house, and this time, I was ready.

This time, I was wearing my oldest trainers, my scuzziest navy tracksuit bottoms and a wine-coloured T-shirt that wouldn't show red-brick dust too much.

"Where are you off to, then?" Mum had asked, as she pinned the damp duvet cover on the washing line (again), and let it flap about over the top of the weeds.

"Going drawing," I'd told her, holding up the nylon rucksack with my pad and pencils in it.

I'd heard a thump behind me, and wondered if Peaches was planning on forsaking his snooze in favour of shadowing me (I decided to stick a custard cream in my pocket, just in case).

It wasn't like I'd made up my mind to come to the house straight away. After I'd given up on Peaches' caricature, my brain had almost played a game of Chinese whispers with itself.

Firstly, I'd fidgeted with the seagull feather – the one I'd saved from the shower and stuck beside the shells.

Secondly, the feather got me thinking about the seagull I'd tried to draw on Monday.

Thirdly, my thoughts meandered on to fairy cakes. (Of course.)

Fourthly, I started musing about fairies (minus cakes), and ended up staring at the delicate watercolour above the desk.

Fifthly, I'd idly started doodling my *own* fairy (only mine looked less like dainty, wispy Victorian sprite and more like twenty-first century Japanese cartoon-style *funky* fairy).

Sixthly, I got distracted from my funky fairy when a shadow fell over the outhouse window, as Mum pinned up my duvet on the line. It was the pawprints that got me thinking – the washing machine might have tumbled the worst of the red stain out of the material, but with the sun shining through you could still make out those faint, peachy pad-marks.

Seventhly (if there is such a word), scrambling up the side of the Josephs' house for a proper peek inside suddenly seemed like the *exact* thing I should do right now.

And so here I was – thanks to Chinese whispers in my head – dumping my bag down by the dandelions and foxgloves and eyeing up the window above me.

With a couple of grunts, a squeak and an "ooof!", I found myself tumbling over the window sill and on to a wooden floor. It took a second or two for my eyes to acclimatize after the dazzle of the day outside, and for me to sit and get my breath back. Slowly, as the duskiness gradually became less dusky to me, I stared around a vast empty room, as big as my old school gym. But disappointingly, there was no furniture, no trailing velvet curtains at the windows, no ornaments or pictures to give any clues about the history of the house and its once-upon-a-time owners. The only signs that the place had ever been grand were a giant marble fireplace at one end of the room, and walls covered in faded, peeling floral wallpaper. This had to have been a ballroom, where the Joseph family and their friends would've waltzed the night away in big, flowing dresses and moustaches (if you see what I mean).

I pushed myself up and walked towards the huge, imposing fireplace, stepping over a wilting daisy chain on the dusty floor that must have blown in here from outside. But my eyes were on a coloured chunk of something glinting in the hearth. It was just the corner of a tile, one of many that must have been here long ago, and the fragment of yellow and green flower glazed on it made me ache to see what the rest of the tiles and the whole of this room must have looked like, back when it was loved, back when. . .

. . .and then in mid-thought, I felt every hair on the back of my neck stand to attention. Maybe it was those electrical impulses up to their tricks again, but I suddenly didn't feel *alone* any more. Slipping the tile into my pocket I turned slowly, slowly and saw tiny, darting *wisps* of colour and light, fluttering in the gently swirling dust my clumsy entrance had created.

Could it. . .

I mean, could it be. . .

Could it be, well, *fairies*. . .?

Were *these* the current tenants of the Josephs' house, now that humans didn't seem to want it?

Uh-oh. I'd come to Portbore and I was going *mad*.

"There's no such thing as fairies," I whispered to myself – and the fairies. But standing there, frozen in shock, I couldn't think of a single explanation for the twinkling dapples of light flurrying and flitting around the room. Or for the tiny, melodic tinkles they seemed to be making.

THUNK!

That wasn't the sound of a fairy, unless it was one who'd borrowed Dad's sledgehammer.

In a panic, I glanced at the furthest away window and saw that a huge gull had landed on the sill and was now settling itself, giving its feathers a shake and eyeing me boldly.

"Caww!" it suddenly cackled, chucking its head back as it squawked.

Like some kind of nervous tic, I almost copied the movement, jerking my chin up a little and then catching sight of . . . the most amazing chandelier I'd ever seen. It was *massive*. The breeze from the open windows was making every one of the hundreds of dangling crystal droplets sway and twist, sending sparkles of kaleidoscopic light dancing around the room.

Ahhhh . . . *now* I got it.

OK, so there *weren't* any real live fairies inhabiting the house. But it didn't matter – my small reserve of courage was fading fast and it was time to leave, before any more tinkles and *THUNK*s frightened me into permanent goosebumps.

"Bye, house," I whispered, hurriedly throwing one leg after another over the window sill, and bounding down on to the warm grass below.

As I grabbed my bag and hurried through the garden, I thought I saw the faintest flicker of something that *might* have been a ginger tail disappearing through the tall grass. But I wasn't in the mood to hang about; if it *was* Peaches, then I'd see him back at home later, where the ear-splitting shrieks of my brothers would keep any spookiness *well* at bay.

But right now, all I wanted was to get to the bustling, tacky beach in Portbore, treat myself to a 99 cone with everything on it, and think about when I might be brave enough to visit the Josephs' house again.

Course I knew that would be the weekend, when the world's most fearless girl would be here to hold my shaking hand. . .

Chapter 15

Nineteenth-century gossip

". . .How I wonder what you are!"

Omigod. If Frankie or Neish or the others could see me now, they'd think I'd gone stark, raving Looncy Tunes.

Sitting on my bedroom window sill, swinging my legs and singing "Twinkle, Twinkle Little Star" to a *cat*? They'd disown me. (If a few of them hadn't disowned me already, by the sound of their silence.)

I know it would have looked a bit wet and Walt Disney to anyone watching, but it was nice sitting up here in the warm dark, with Peaches purring companionably by my side. We'd watched the sun set over the sea together, and the lights strung along the prom ping to life. Then – like quiet fireworks – a blaze of coloured bulbs sparked up down by the beach. The official opening of the funfair was the next day, Friday, but I guess the people who ran it knew that there was no better advert than to flick their very big "on" switch.

Then, as if nature was trying to outdo Portbore, a few wisps of clouds floated off to reveal a nearly whole moon and a galaxy of stars.

That's when I got it into my head to sing "Twinkle, Twinkle". And anyway, the line "How I wonder what you are" seemed kind of weirdly appropriate when I was warbling it to Peaches. . .

"Hey, I thought you were scared of heights?" Dad's voice drifted from the doorway behind me.

"Not any more." I turned around and smiled.

"Good! Anyway, if you fell, Peaches would probably cushion your fall!" he laughed, coming over and leaning his long, muscly arms on the window sill beside me.

"Are you saying he's fat?" I asked, wrapping a protective arm around Peaches and pretending to be offended.

"Hey, I guess he's not fat . . . for a baby hippopotamus!"

I took my hand away from Peaches' broad back and gave my dad a punch on the arm.

"Ooh! I take it back, I take it back!" Dad said, acting like I'd hurt him, though he'd had harder punches (not to mention nippier bites) from my little brothers. "Please don't set Peaches' fleas on me! *Please!*"

"Did you come in here to be annoying, or did you have another reason?" I asked, raising my eyebrows at him.

"To be annoying," he grinned, falling down on to his knees and resting his chin on his hands. "As well as the *other* reason, of course."

Before I asked him what that other reason was, I took a quick peek at my dad and realized he looked . . . well . . . not like my dad. *My* dad wore expensive suits and trendy ties. *My* dad managed to look dressed up, even off-duty in jeans, wearing them with "casual" shirts and shoes, never trainers. *My* dad was forty, with a frown permanently in place on his forehead. But *this* dad; *this* dad looked like his clothes had never been introduced to an iron. *This* dad had a T-shirt with Nirvana written on it. *This* dad had been smiling so much the last few days that he was going to give himself laughter lines, but there wasn't a forehead frown in sight.

"So? What's your other reason?" I asked, waving a curious moth away from my face.

"I got talking to one of our neighbours today. Her name's Maggie – she's a retired teacher who moved to Portbay ten years ago."

Why was Dad telling me this? Had he arranged something hideous, like for me to have extra tutorials with her over the summer holidays?

"Anyway, I was asking her about the old couple who used to own this place," he continued.

OK, maybe I was safe. This didn't sound like it was leading to holiday tutoring. I already knew that Foxglove Cottage used to belong to an old couple who'd moved into a retirement home or something. It had been left to grow damp and crumbly for a few years, till the owners' son decided to sell up. (Bet no one in the town would touch it with a bargepole; bet he had to wait till the mugs from London with more-money-than-sense came along. . .)

"So?" I prompted him, while Peaches lazily swatted at the moth with one enormo paw.

"*So*. . ." Dad waffled on, ". . .she was saying that the few years she knew the couple who lived here, she never heard them talk about art, or saw them drawing."

"Then whoever owned the cottage *before* them must have used the outhouse as a studio!" I suggested, not having to try *too* hard to work that one out.

"Uh-huh." Dad nodded and agreed. "But it

would have been a long, long time ago. Maggie said the old guy had lived in it all his life. He'd been born here, just after his parents bought the place."

How amazing – to spend all your life in the same house, to live out all your history in one place. Maybe it *wasn't* such a crummy idea to do the place up after all. But who was the mystery artist who'd used the outhouse as a studio? By the old-fashioned look of the fairy painting, the ancient art materials and the fragile felt hat, I realized something.

"So I guess the artist must have been someone who –" I began, stopping to check that the maths I'd done in my head was right, "– who must've lived in the house maybe as much as a hundred years ago!"

"I guess so," Dad nodded, casting his grey-blue eyes up to the stars outside in the night sky. "Anyway, Maggie told me some interesting things about the town, too."

"Oh, yeah?" I said warily, wondering if Dad was using the excuse of this chat to give me a subtle lecture about Portbore's good points.

"Yeah. Lots of smuggling and piracy went on round here centuries ago, y'know!"

"I *do* know," I told him matter-of-factly. The mad old dear with the fairy cake had already filled me in on *that* particular snippet of local history.

"And she said we have to check out a place called Sugar Bay."

I didn't say anything, but was aware of a pair of green eyes glancing up at me.

"She says it's a beautiful little cove, just on the other side of the caravan park on the headland," Dad carried on, unaware that I knew it pretty well. "There's an old, dilapidated mansion there, apparently; built by some rich plantation owner in eighteen-hundred-and-something, who settled here from Barbados. Guess he must have made his fortune in the sugar trade."

Peaches had looked dopey and sleepy for most of the time I'd known him so far, but I swear his ears did a three-hundred-and-sixty-degree swivel right then – same as *mine* would have, if I had swivelling kind of ears.

"That must be why it's called Sugar Bay!" I gasped, the realization dawning on me, as vivid as the sun zooming back up in the sky and nudging the moon out of the way.

"I suppose so!" Dad agreed, nodding at me. "Anyway, *here's* a bit of interesting historical gossip for you: the plantation owner and his family caused quite a stir in Portbay at the time because they brought a young black servant boy back with them from the Caribbean."

"Really?" I murmured, feeling goosebumps prickling all over my skin at that piece of information.

"Mad, isn't it, to think that some teenage boy was the talk of the town, just because of the colour of his skin!" Dad laughed. "Mind you, a glimpse of a lady's ankle would have been front page news in those days!"

Ha! The citizens of Portbore didn't just get their knickers in a twist over nothing in the nineteenth century – hadn't the sight of my stripy socks sent a ripple of *shock* around Shingles café just the other day?

"Anyway . . . this time tomorrow, Frankie will be here!" said Dad brightly, changing the subject. "Looking forward to it?"

"Oh, yes," I grinned, forgetting all my niggling worries about my best friend.

After all, when Frankie breezed into town, frumpy Portbore wouldn't know what had hit it. . .

Chapter 16

Mrs Sticky Toffee and the tooth fairy

Tippety-tap, tippety-tap, tippety-tippety-tippety-tap!

What was making that sound? It took me a few minutes to work it out.

Tippety-tap, tippety-tap, tippety-tippety-tippety-tap!

Libraries are meant to be silent, right? Well, not this one. A small transistor radio on the shelf behind the desk was tuned into some station that should've been called Crummy FM, and corny old Frank Sinatra was currently crooning out a tune (help – I felt homesick for Clive our singing neighbour!).

Not only was Frank crooning, but the librarian – busy putting away a pile of books – was keeping time by *tap*-dancing his way between the shelves. (*Tippety-tap, tippety-tap, tippety-tippety-tippety-tap. . .!*)

Nuts. Seriously nuts.

Still, the backgound noise was a blessing in

disguise – you'd never notice me snoring with all that racket going on. And I was *seriously* in danger of snoring for two reasons. First, I'd hardly slept last night 'cause of Peaches snoring, Frankie coming and thinking about that servant boy from Sugar Bay and the hard time he'd got in this town. Second, the book I was flicking through was as boring as watching my dad strip wallpaper in the hall (his riveting project for today).

Point of Interest No. 3: The crazy golf course – with its Treasure Island theme – has been popular with locals and tourists alike since it opened in 1962.

What a dazzlingly fascinating fact (not). Good grief – it might be home to loads of weirdos, but this town was obviously *so* boring that no one had bothered to write a decent history of it.

I mean, get this; I was sitting at a desk in the library with the one, single, solitary guidebook to Portbore, and I'd read leaflets about plaque at the *dentist* that were thicker than this. It was full of these "Points of Interest" that were about as interesting as a verruca. What other thrilling points of interest could I expect?

*. . .No. 51: The third lamppost on the left
as you walk along the prom has long been a
favourite with local dogs.*

As for the one place I was dying to know more
about. . .

*Point of interest No. 5: Sugar Bay – Once
known as Smuggler's Bay, due to the fact that
this hidden cove was perfect for smugglers
unloading their stolen wares. Its name was
changed when the Grainger family moved
from Barbados to the area and in 1840 built
a grand house with the profits of the fortune
they'd built in the sugar trade.*

And that was *it*! No info about the family, *or*
their servant, or why exactly the house had been
left to moulder away. They hadn't even got the
family name right – what was with "Grainger"
instead of "Joseph"?

What a waste of time. I hadn't written a *thing*
in the notepad I'd taken along; instead of jotting
down fascinating historical facts, I'd just covered
the pages in *doodles*. It was Mum who'd suggested
that I come to the library to learn more about the

Josephs' house, but I think I'd learned *less* (if that was possible), *and* got more confused into the bargain.

"Ooh, now *that's* more like it!" said a familiar voice close by, as I was enveloped in a whiff of toffee. It reminded me of happy, sticky days eating sticky toffee pudding with Frankie in Aunt Esme's cosy kitchen.

"Um . . . hello!" I said shyly, turning to see the old woman from the beach. Against the dark wood of the bookshelves her lime-green coat and pink meringue hat looked more vivid than ever.

"You know, that's *so* much prettier than the style you were doing before!" the old lady smiled, not bothering with a hello herself.

Her dainty cream handbag swinging from her wrist, she tapped a wrinkled finger on one of my doodles. It wasn't bad, actually; it was another of my funky fairies, complete with dragonfly-meets-Batman wings.

"Don't know about that cropped top and tummy button ring, though!" she murmured, turning her head this way and that as she studied my drawing. "But I guess I'm just a bit out of touch with the fashions that fairies are wearing these days!"

Was that an attempt at a joke, or was she just

mad? To be polite, I forced a smile. I figured that if she'd been joking, then it was the right response, and if she was plain mad, then it was probably the safest thing to do.

"So, what's this?" she queried now, breathing toffee fumes over me as she shifted her gaze to the so-called book I'd been flicking through. "Doing some homework about your new home town?"

Urgh. I didn't want to think of this as homework and I didn't much want to think of Portbore being my new home town either, thank you very much.

"I was trying to find out about the Joseph family and their servant," I told her, pointing to the poor-quality black-and-white print of the old house at Sugar Bay.

Mrs Sticky Toffee frowned for a second and then had an "aha!" moment. "Ah, now, you're barking up the wrong kettle of fish, there, dear!" she announced. "The family weren't called Joseph; they were the Graingers – Mr and Mrs Grainger and their daughter Elize."

So the book had been right *after* all? Hey, now I was even *more* confused. "But why is it called the Josephs' house, then?" I blinked at her.

"It's not *the Josephs*', dear – it's just *Joseph*, as in, Joseph's house. The locals have always referred to it as that in honour of the Grainger's servant, Joseph."

"Really?" I asked in surprise, wondering how I could have been so dumb as to mishear the name in such a small but important way.

"Oh, yes! Of course, back in those days, practically no one had set eyes on a black person before. The townspeople of Portbay were terribly proud to be the first place on the south coast to have someone of colour in their midst. He was quite the celebrity!"

Well, knock me down with a seagull feather. Last night, I'd been tossing and turning, thinking that poor servant boy had been made to feel like an outsider, some kind of *freak* here, and all the time the locals had thought of him as *special*. Special enough to call the old house at Sugar Bay after him, and not the master who'd built it. Wow.

I was about to ask why, if Joseph was so famous, there was nothing in the local library about him, but with a rustle of her raincoat, Mrs Sticky Toffee was on the move.

"Oops! Would you look at the time . . . I'll be late for my appointment to get my bunions done!"

Er, I hadn't a clue what bunions were exactly,

and I didn't know what you might get *done* to them, but whatever – they sure didn't sound like something I'd want to know about. Just as she was heading for the door, Mrs Sticky Toffee glanced over her shoulder – almost catching me wincing – and said. . .

"If you want to know more about Joseph's house, have a look in the museum, dear!"

Museum? I didn't even know Portbore *had* a museum. But then it seemed like there was plenty about Portbore that I didn't know about. . .

And then I remembered my manners and went to wave bye . . . but Mrs Sticky Toffee had already vanished, off to get her bunions "done". (Bleurghh. . .)

"I hope she's not the tooth fairy!" a man's voice cheerfully announced. It was the tap-dancing librarian, hovering beside me with an armful of books.

"Excuse me?" I asked, completely stumped.

"Well, she shouldn't be offering sweets if she's the tooth fairy, should she!" he beamed at me, before click-clacking off to the desk to stamp someone's book out.

Was that another sort of strange joke? Or another sign of madness?

Just as I was trying to decide which one it was, I spotted something on my notepad. I'd doodled my funky fairy with arms outstretched, and now she seemed to be holding something out to me.

"Er, thanks," I mumbled to no one in particular, as I picked up the toffee and started unwrapping it. . .

Chapter 17

The truth about the texts (or lack of 'em)

My heart was in my mouth.

I'd missed her call from the train – my mobile had gone missing and only reappeared when Dad was lassoing Jamie into the double buggy beside Jake and felt the unusual bump in Jamie's nappy.

"Hi – s'me! Frankie! I'm on the train now, and I think it's running on time, so see you at half-six!" I'd heard her say, once I'd given the phone a wipe with a Wet One and listened to my messages.

It had been chaos when I'd come back from the library this afternoon. I'd planned to spend a bit of time making my room look less like a half-built hovel for Frankie coming, but instead I'd had to help wash and brush away Jamie and Jake's latest disaster. When Mum had put the washing on, she hadn't spotted the twins adding the entire contents of the box of washing powder – plus the box – into the porthole door of our Zanussi. Actually, the first Mum and Dad knew about the mutant foam tidal wave that was oozing out of our drain, down the driveway and covering a whole section of Dingle Lane was when I ran in and told them. (I'd been walking up the lane on the way home and couldn't figure out why cars were coming towards me covered in floaty layers of foamy bubbles.)

So, *first* there was the big clear-up, and then there was *another* panic when Dad tried to blow up the inflatable spare bed and found he couldn't 'cause Jamie had bitten straight through the rubber tube of the pump. Dad had tried to repair it with tape, but it didn't work – the bed flopped limply across the floor, as if a hamster with asthma had tried (and failed) to blow it up. He went next door to see if our neighbour Maggie happened to have a spare pump (or failing that, a spare cage for the twins), and ended up wheeling back a fold-out single bed that she'd been happy to lend us.

By the time he'd dragged it upstairs to my room, we were already late leaving for the station. Then we were later *still* 'cause I had to run indoors to find a Wet One for my phone. I guess we must have really looked like the Barking Mad Family from London as we raced along the road in the direction of the station, Dad pushing a double buggy of squealing, delighted boys at top speed.

We needn't have hurried. The train turned out to be running ten minutes late, due to the wrong sort of track on the track or something. Actually, it was a pity Frankie's train had been held up, because for the first time today I'd had time to worry. No sooner did my heart rate start to slow down after our sprint to get here, then it started tappity-tapping faster than a librarian's shoes at the thought of how exactly Frankie was going to *be*. 'Cause no matter how much my mum tried to stick up for her, Frankie had acted so off-hand on the phone and by e-mail this week, that I wasn't sure what to expect. Only her cheeky postcard had sounded like the Frankie I knew and adored. So which Frankie was going to get off the train. . .?

It didn't take long to spot her – amongst a sea of bobbing, white-haired pensioners stepping on to the platform, you couldn't really miss a pretty black teenage girl with tiny braids flying as she ran full tilt, arms outstretched, yelling, "Stell-*AAAAAAAA*!". . .

*

"WOOOOF!" barked Jake. "WOOF! WOOF! WOOF!"

The big hairy Alsatian tied up in front of the

café just about jumped out of its hairy skin, but I think that was less to do with my brother's "uncanny" dog impersonation and more to do with the fact that Jake was slamming his hands over and over again against the plate-glass window.

Some concerned-looking bloke behind the counter – who might have been the owner of the Shingles café – appeared to be as alarmed as the dog outside on the pavement. They weren't the only ones; every customer in the place on this busy Friday night was staring at us. I was just glad I was facing the window and had my back to their disapproving glances.

"Wanna see the DOGGIE!" Jake yelled above the sound of his heavy-duty glass thumping.

"I'd better take him outside; try and calm him down a bit," Dad mumbled, screeching his chair back and making a grab for Jake.

"Hmm," Mum nodded wearily.

She was doing her best to seem cheery for Frankie's sake, but the boys efforts at causing maximum mayhem today had kind of ground her down, I suspected.

"Can you girls keep an eye on Jamie while I nip to the loo?" Mum asked, once the café door had clanged shut behind Dad and Jake.

"Sure. . ." I nodded, wishing Mum and Dad hadn't decided to take us straight here for a "treat" instead of going home for our tea.

"No problem!" Frankie smiled at Mum, chomping on her last mouthful of carbonara.

But before Mum had got two steps from the table, a terrible wailing started up.

"Mummmmee-EEEEEEEE!" sobbed Jamie, holding out his arms as if she was abandoning him to the Childcatcher from *Chitty Chitty Bang Bang* instead of his own sister.

Once Mum had sighed, grabbed Jamie and trundled off to the loo with him on her hip, Frankie rolled her eyes and grinned at me.

"Couldn't you trade 'em in for something quieter, like a couple of goldfish, maybe?" she joked, even though she'd known the twins since they were two days old and thought they were pretty entertaining, really.

"Don't suggest that to Mum – the mood she's in today, she'd probably think that was an ace idea!" I joked back.

This was great. Not the boys showing us up, I mean – just Frankie being here, and . . . well . . . being Frankie. I needn't have worried about how she'd react to me when she stepped off the train;

the second I felt her hug the breath out of me on the station platform I knew we'd be fine. And in between Jake and Jamie's food fights, fist fights and screaming matches here in the café, me, Frankie, Mum and Dad had jabbered away like crazy, catching up on news of the move and how Aunt Esme was doing and loads more.

Course, in front of Mum and Dad, I didn't moan too much about the boringness of Portbore, and Frankie didn't ask – but there'd be plenty of time to catch up on that later, when we were on our own.

"What are *that* lot staring at?" Frankie suddenly frowned over my shoulder. I turned around and saw a bunch of about five teenage lads at the back of the caff, huddled around Cokes, grinning and staring our way.

"I was going to tell you about them!" I turned back and whispered across the table, though there was no way the boys could have heard me above the din of the music from the jukebox, the chattering of families and the violent hiss of the coffee machine. "I'm *sure* they're the same lads that were in here on Sunday, taking the mickey out of me!"

"Oh, yeah?" Frankie bristled. "Well, we'd better

give them something to look at, then!"

Uh-oh. With Frankie, you never knew what to expect. I felt a familiar flutter of panic as I watched her stand up – dressed in a white vest top and pink combats – and wondered momentarily if I had time to bolt outside or slither under the table before she did whatever she was going to do.

But just like always, fear froze my muscles and I wasn't going *anywhere*. Instead, I watched as Frankie put one hand on her hip and blew the most exaggerated kiss in the lads' direction with the other. Ha!

I *had* to see their reaction. Sneaking a backward peek, I spotted a couple of them pull faces and give embarrassed laughs, but Frankie's full-on cheekiness had done the trick. Every one of the lads had turned awkwardly away from us and started looking very interested in the table.

"*That* was easy!" Frankie said with satisfaction, sliding gracefully back on to her seat, and stealing an uneaten carrot off Jamie's plate. "Boys can never handle girls who are more full-on than them. So . . . who do you want me to sort out for you next, Stella?"

Frankie pulled her knees up and rested her trainers on the table, biting the end off the carrot with a loud crunch.

"Um, no one, I don't think," I said, realizing that the only people I really knew so far in Portbore were Mrs Sticky Toffee and Peaches, and Peaches didn't really count as a person (or a normal *cat*). "But hey, I wanted to ask you, Frankie ... what's going on with Lauren and Eleni and Parminder?"

At the mention of our other friends' names, Frankie stopped crunching and dropped her feet back down on the floor with a thud.

"What do you – *cuh* – mean?" she asked, choking slightly on her carrot.

"Well, it's just that I've tried phoning them and they never get back to my messages, or my texts or e-mails. I mean, I heard from Neish – like I told you in my e-mail, she texted me about some gossip or something on Tuesday, but I haven't heard from her since. . ."

Frankie looked positively weird for a second, like one of those policemen on TV shows that arrives to break bad news but faffs around before spitting it out.

"What?" I laughed nervously. "Have they all been abducted by aliens or run off and joined a cult or something? Is *that* why they've been so lousy at keeping in touch?"

The fooling around there; that was just my way of trying to keep calm . . . I could feel the flutter of a stammer threatening.

And then finally Frankie spoke.

"The thing is, Stella," she said with a sigh, staring off at the waitresses stacking dirty trays on the counter. "They've felt funny about speaking to you."

"Funny? Funny *how*?" I blinked at her, flutters of panic rattling around in my chest again.

Frankie shuffled in her seat looking uncomfortable, like she was struggling to come up with an answer to my question, or just finding it hard to say the answer out loud. "Funny, 'cause they know something . . . and don't want to be the one to tell you."

I didn't like the sound of that one tiny, little bit.

"What? What *sort* of something?"

Frankie frowned, and my heart flopped even nearer to the floor.

"It's just that . . . well . . . it's *Seb* – OK?" She was staring at me now, sort of annoyed, as if I'd forced her to do something she didn't want to do.

"O-O-O-OK," I mumbled, feeling very, *very* far

from OK myself.

For a split-second, I almost started nervously joking again; nearly asked if it was *Seb* who'd been abducted by aliens or run off to join a cult or something terrible like that. . .

"Look, Stell – he's going out with someone. None of the girls wanted to be the one to break the news to you. They knew you'd be gutted."

Neisha nearly did, but must have lost her bottle after she texted me, I thought numbly for a second, as the news sank in.

Outside, I could see Dad hovering warily, as Jake patted/thumped the nervy Alsatian on the head. And the bellowed roar of "IWANAN-ICECREAM!" coming from the direction of the loos meant that Mum and Jamie were on their way back to the table. But it was as if I could see and hear my family through a fog – Frankie's words were the only thing I could concentrate on, like they were TeChNiCoLoUr in my head.

"Wh-wh-wh-who is she?" I asked, sounding like a puzzled owl, not a traumatized 13-year-old girl.

"No one," shrugged Frankie, ducking away from a waitress – the grumpy red-haired one I'd seen before – as she started clearing away the plates. "Just some girl. She was hanging around Seb the night after your party – we saw them up at the Heath."

So *that's* why she'd kept Saturday night a secret. Like Mum had suggested, Frankie was only trying to protect me.

"You all right, Stella?" she asked, biting her lip.

I was just about to answer her when a ball of lightning dressed in Gap Kids jeans hurtled into the waitress's legs, sending her – and the stacked tray she was carrying – flying.

"*Jamie!* Look what you've *done*!!" I heard Mum's shocked voice shout out.

Gazing across the table, I could *just* about see Frankie's face through the strands of soggy spaghetti that were dangling in front of my eyes. She was trying really, *really* hard not to laugh.

"Say sorry to the poor waitress *right* now, Jamie!" Mum ordered my brother.

"Sowwy, lady!"

"*And* your sister!"

"Sowwy, Stewwa!"

Ignoring Jamie's apology, I watched – through eyelashes dripping with white sauce – Frankie's shoulders heave as she struggled to keep her sniggers in.

"Hey, Frankie," I suddenly asked her. "What

were you saying about me being all right?"

And with that, she exploded, sending infectious giggles splurging across the table and setting me off too.

After all, it was hard to stay tearful and tragic with leftover carbonara dolloped on your head.

Though in its *own* way, that was pretty tragic too. . .

Chapter 18

Sad, sad, sad or funny, funny, funny?

"You have *got* to be kidding!" Frankie growled.

"Yo ho ho! Yo ho ho!" a jovial voice replied.

"I'm sorry, Stella, but I'd rather eat my own *arm* than go in there!"

"In there" was the Treasure Island crazy golf course.

"Yo ho ho! Yo ho ho!"

"I don't know what *he's* 'yo ho ho'-ing at!" Frankie grumbled, staring at the life-size fibre-glass pirate in front of us. "They should change the tape in the machine so he says 'sad, sad, sad', 'cause that's what this place is!"

"I dunno!" I laughed. "It's pretty funny, Frankie!"

From what we could see of the golf course over the perimeter hedge, it was packed full of miniature galleons, gaudy treasure chests, plastic palm trees and lots of people having a laugh. One little kid nearby was cheering his dad on as he

174

putted a golf ball into the mouth of a pirate who was buried up to the neck in sand. Another kid was stroking the parrot sitting on the shoulder of a mean Captain Hook-a-like. A guy in his twenties was groaning as his golf ball disappeared into a shark-infested puddle. It hadn't been my idea to come here – Dad had dropped us off on his way to a timber yard he'd heard about – but now that I could see it for myself, I suddenly understood why the crazy golf course had been so "popular with locals and tourists alike" for the last however many years. Yeah, it was totally naff, but kind of cute too.

"*Funny*? Are you having me on, Stell?!" Frankie pulled a horrified face. "This place is as corny as Kellogg's Cornflakes!"

Er . . . wasn't that the point? For it to be corny, I mean? Crazy golf was hardly ultra cool or cutting-edge. What did Frankie expect? A *Matrix*-themed course, with state-of-the-art special effects and a full-size statue of Keanu Reeves saying "I am Neo"? Still, I didn't say all that stuff out loud to Frankie. She was in one of those moods where everything (and everyone) was fair game for a sarky put-down. Normally I didn't mind them – the moods or the sarky put-downs – 'cause they were pretty entertaining. But today I was feeling sort of sensitive, I guess: the news about Seb had left me with an ache in my chest, as if I had a big, tender bruise on my heart. . .

I really wanted to talk to Frankie about all that again, but hadn't had the chance since she first blurted it out to me in the café yesterday. Thing was, once we'd got home last night, I ended up suspecting that my parents were missing the company of their friends more than just a little bit, 'cause they *sure* made a fuss of mine. They hardly left me and Frankie alone for a minute. I mean, OK, it *had* been a laugh: all of us showing her around the house (Dad posed cheesily with his sledgehammer), eating ice-cream (Mum took out the good Ben & Jerry's stuff once the twins were safely asleep), and sniggering about the spaghetti incident (it *was* funny, though I didn't plan on going back to the Shingles café for the next century or so). But by bedtime, I was aching to get Frankie on my own, to finally get a chance to talk about Seb and the girl who'd turned his head two seconds after I'd left town. But when I came back to my room after brushing my teeth, Frankie was already asleep – arms, legs and braids flung star-shaped across the borrowed single bed.

I'd stayed awake in the dark for ages after that, curled up on the top of the duvet, staring out through my open window at the spangles of lights from the funfair down at the beach. The whole time, running through my mind like the lyrics of some song, was, *Hey, bad timing! Love S xxx* . . . the message scrawled on the back of the mangled Polaroid. I didn't get to sleep till Peaches silently bounded through the window, snuggled himself into a cosy circle behind my knees, and soothed me with his purry snores.

And then after breakfast this morning, I sneaked Frankie away from her fan club (i.e. my family) and took her out to check out my den. I thought *that* would be the perfect place to have a little privacy and discuss the Seb situation, but I got the feeling Frankie didn't want to. Straight away, she was off – grinning, noseying, teasing, filling the conversation with so many jokes and jibes that there wasn't *space* to change the subject.

"Wow!" she'd gasped, when I'd shoved open the stiff door and ushered her into the den. "What a dump! Hey, isn't this where the plague started?"

"God, what a swot you are!" she'd announced, staring at the sheet of paper I'd printed off the website about Barbados and pinned on my corkboard. "Doing history homework in the holidays? You're mental!"

"Now, Stell," she'd grinned, grabbing the floppy felt hat off its nail and plonking it on her head, "I *know* you're not as hip to fashion as me and Neish and everyone, but honestly, granny chic? I don't *think* so!"

"What's this?" she'd asked, picking up the chunk of tile I'd taken from Joseph's house as a souvenir. "Are you turning into one of those mad old women you see on telly documentaries who hoard junk? *They've* always got skanky, manky cats too!"

She's mucking around and slagging off Peaches 'cause she's just trying to make me laugh and keep my mind off Seb, I'd realized, as I watched Frankie warily pick up the chipped rose-patterned cup and study it like she was examining a test tube full of snot. . .

"Stella," Frankie said sternly now, resting a hand on the face of the "yo-ho-ho"-ing pirate, "*please* tell me there's something more exciting to do in this town!"

"Um. . ." I mumbled, looking off down the prom for inspiration and not finding any. I guess I *could* have suggested paddling with the pensioners or feeding fairy cakes to seagulls, but Frankie probably would have snorted in my face.

"Oh, poor Stella!" Frankie suddenly sighed, stepping away from the pirate and coming over to wrap her arms around me. "You really *have* moved to the most boring place on earth, haven't you. . .?"

I felt a bit dizzy, then realized I'd been holding my breath. (Idiot.)

Taking a big lungful of air now, I watched fascinated as dust swirled around our ankles – not 'cause it was dust, but because I realized it might have lain undisturbed here for *years*. Me and Frankie, we were treading up the creaky, once-grand sweep of stairs, and excitement was fizzling up my spine like bubbles in a fish tank. This was much, *much* further than I'd got before. In a few seconds, we'd be discovering whatever secrets there were to discover in the upstairs rooms, and I couldn't *wait*.

Frankie, meanwhile, couldn't care *less*.

". . .so anyway, they're all going down to Camden Market this afternoon, and get this – Lauren's going to try and pretend to be sixteen, 'cause she's dying to get her belly-button pierced and the place there won't do you under sixteen unless your parents are up for it, and you *know* what Lauren's parents are like!"

I'd decided to show Frankie that Portbore wasn't *totally* boring, and brought her to Sugar Bay, to Joseph's house. Now we were here, I got the feeling that she thought exploring an old decrepit building was about as interesting as finding out how cement's made.

"Eleni said she'd do Lauren's make-up for her to make her look older, but Neish said no, that's a dead giveaway. She's right, isn't she? 'Cause it *does* look like you're trying too hard if you wear loads of make-up, doesn't it? Specially in the daytime!"

"Yeah, I s'pose," I muttered, turning my head this way and that as we reached the first-floor landing and saw several doorways leading off it.

"Parminder's got a bet on with Neisha that Lauren doesn't get away with it," Frankie chatted on, leaning her elbows on the banisters while I darted off to look in each room, where I found nothing but emptiness, bare floorboards and great views from the windows in every one of them.

Over the years, someone – lots of someones? – had obviously stripped out anything original to the house or personal to the family, and I couldn't believe how sad and disappointed that made me feel.

"If Parminder wins, Neisha's got to buy her a copy of *Heat* every week for a month," Frankie babbled away from the landing, "and if *Neisha* wins, she gets to borrow Parminder's hair straighteners for a fortnight."

Only vaguely listening to my best friend, I found myself in the smallest of the bedrooms, as bare and empty as the others. I was about to turn and leave when I spotted something that made me start . . . and then smile. In America, taking a "kitty-corner" is a phrase that means not taking the obvious, straight-ahead route. I think it has to be named after cats, the way they weave their way across a garden, like their paws are following some twisty path that's invisible to the human eye. Well, some cat (some fat ginger cat?) had been kitty-cornering its way right across this room – pawprints lightly stamping a winding trail through the dust over to the window. So I followed, doing some kitty-cornering of my own. (It was just as well that Frankie couldn't see me, or she'd think I'd gone completely barking and jump on the first train out of here. . .)

"Anyway, Lauren was saying that it was a pity

I couldn't go with them today," Frankie's voice drifted through, "'cause if she bottles out, the rest of them will just let her get away with it, but if *I* was there, she'd be too scared not to do it!"

Resting my hands on the window sill, I stared out at the most amazing view of sea, sand, sky and whirling seagulls, and my head went completely buzzy at the idea that someone – long, long, *long* ago – had slept in this room and woken up to this exact same view every day.

"Hey, what're you doing?" asked Frankie, her footsteps now stalking me into the room. "Listen, no offence, Stell, but this place is a bit of a snooze. Can we go somewhere else?"

Just as she spoke, my fingertips sensed grooves in the sill. I glanced down, and saw a name . . . and then another; decades-old graffiti carved in the painted wood. In wobbly, swooping lettering, I made out the first name: *Elize*. The second was *Joseph*. Alongside there was fainter etching that was harder to read.

"'Friends for eternity, 1841'," I mumbled, my heartbeat thundering like it was in training for the hundred metre sprint at the Olympics.

"What?" mumbled Frankie, through a yawn.

"Listen, I know somewhere else we can go!" I

grinned, ignoring her question.

"Oh, yeah? Where?"

"The museum!"

"You have *got* to be kidding!" Frankie growled, for the second time today. . .

Chapter 19

A feeling of déjà view. . .

"Look at the *state* of this! Did that minging cat of yours sleep in my overnight bag or something?" moaned Frankie, picking rogue ginger hairs off her black sleeveless top.

I'd been charging ahead of her, along corridors packed with cabinets of blunderbusses, nabbed loot, and general gruesome info about smugglers and pirates (all to be looked at another time, when I wasn't so distracted). But at the mention of Peaches I stopped, and let Frankie catch up.

"Hey, what are you doing, you nutter!" she laughed at me.

A family studying pirate paraphernalia started staring at *us* instead of the exhibits. Maybe it was because Frankie was dressed like she was a dancer for a particularly cool R'n'B act, and would have looked more at home on *MTV* than in Portbore Museum. Or maybe it was because I was sniffing her top. . .

"Nope, Peaches definitely didn't sleep on your stuff," I told her, detecting no telltale sweet scent.

"Better watch out!" said Frankie, nodding towards the puzzled family. "They'll call security and get us chucked out!"

"What – for inappropriate Sniffing of Clothes in a Public Place?" I joked back, straightening up and heading off along the corridors at high speed again.

"Er ... what exactly are we looking for?" Frankie panted, struggling to keep up with me.

"Not sure – but I'll know it when I find it," I said vaguely.

And then I nearly missed it, I was hurrying so much. But *something* made me pause in one particular doorway. Slowly – forgetting to breathe again for a second – I stepped inside, staring all around me at this strangely familiar room, with its wine-coloured, flocked wallpaper and ornate antique furniture.

"So? What's this, then?" asked Frankie, stumbling in behind me.

I was pretty certain I knew what it was, but went over to check out the plaque on the wall anyway.

"'Ballroom, circa 1850'," I read out the heading. "'This grand room was replicated from Joseph's house, Sugar Bay, using antiques and artefacts taken from the original building.'"

"All I heard was *Ballroom blah, blah, blah. . .*" Frankie shrugged. "D'you fancy translating?"

"It's a room from the house we've just come from!" I explained excitedly, to a frankly unimpressed Frankie.

Actually, it was the huge room I'd first scrambled into, earlier in the week. But instead of just dust, daisy chains and dapples of light, there was a grand piano, swanky velvet sofas, paintings on the wall and tall candlesticks on the fireplace.

"Look!" I gasped, hurrying over to the marble fireplace and gazing down at the flowery yellow and green glazed tiles in the hearth.

"OK, I'm looking at a *floor* . . . so what am I supposed to see exactly?"

"Those tiles! There's the chipped one – I've got the corner of that on my desk, beside the shells!" I carried on, ignoring Frankie's lack of enthusiasm.

Poor Frankie – she and museums went together like mince and trifle. We'd passed the Shingles café on the way; I should have left her there with a copy of *CosmoGirl* and a doughnut till I was done here.

"Omigod . . . Frankie! Check it out!" I suddenly gasped, staring up at the family portrait hanging above the fireplace. "It's *them*! In *this* room! I mean, the *real* room!"

"'The Grainger family, 1840'," Frankie read from the brass plate next to the painting. "Great. Anyway, listen . . . I saw a seat out in the corridor and my feet are tired with all this rushing around. So I'll meet you there, yeah?"

I think I said yeah, or fine or whatever, but I was too busy gawping at the sight of the stern-looking Victorian parents posed on the sofa, with a pretty dark-haired girl standing obediently behind them. It *had* to be their daughter Elize, and she must have been about ten. And in the background, holding a tray, was a boy not much older, in a red velvet jacket with brass buttons. Joseph. . .

I stared at the two young faces – one dark-skinned, one light – and tried to figure out the feelings going on behind them. The boy Joseph might have been holding an upright, uptight pose, but the painter had made his dark brown eyes bright and alive. Same with Elize's earnest expression – her mouth might not have been smiling but her eyes sure were.

"Lovely painting, isn't it?"

The voice belonged to a woman in a navy blazer. Spotting the "curator" badge on her lapel, I panicked for a second, thinking that Frankie had been right and we were about to be chucked out. Or maybe she'd heard me saying the thing about the tile and was going to demand I hand it over.

"Do you know the house?" she asked, not seeming to mind that I was staring at her like a fool in my panic.

"Mmm," I nodded nervously.

"The museum was very lucky that Miss Grainger donated the contents of this room when she finally moved out – everything else had to be sold. Vandals have made a bit of a mess of what little was left, I'm afraid!"

"Miss Grainger. . . That's the girl, isn't it? Elize?" I asked, curiosity getting the better of my nerves, now that I realized the curator hadn't heard a word I'd said to Frankie, *or* had any plans to order me to collect my loud friend and *leave*.

"Elize, yes!" she beamed, looking as chuffed as my old maths teacher did when I managed to figure out a percentage problem without taking as long as normal (i.e. *for ever*).

"So why did she move out?"

"Well, when she was young, her father gambled away most of the family fortune, and it was always a struggle to keep the house going after that. But Elize – Miss Grainger – somehow managed for years, until it finally became too much for her. She moved away in 1900, when she was quite an old lady – she was about 70, I think."

"What happened to her after that?"

"She moved to a small cottage in the town. It must have been very upsetting for her to see her former home go to rack and ruin after that."

So now I knew what had happened to Elize. But what about her "eternal" friend?

"And what about the servant boy – Joseph?" I asked tentatively.

The curator woman seemed very impressed with my local knowledge. I half-expected her to give me a certificate or a gold star or a *hug* or something. Still, all I was interested in was finding out if Elize and Joseph stayed as close as they were when they were children, back when they carved their names in what must have been Elize's bedroom, just a year after this portrait was painted.

"Joseph? Well, Mr Grainger left him some money when he died. It was enough for Joseph to give up working at the house and leave Portbay.

He was still only a teenager, and I suppose he wanted to see something of the world."

"And nobody heard from him again?" I asked, thinking fleetingly of my grandad, Eddie.

"I don't think so," the curator shook her head. "But people in the town were rather sorry he'd left. They started referring to the old place as Joseph's house after that, even though Miss Grainger and her mother still lived there."

So "eternity" had turned out to be pretty short-lived for Elize and Joseph. But then I supposed that if people gave my Nana Jones and Grandad Eddie a hard time for dating in the 1950s, then how hard would it have been for the servant and the master's daughter to be buddies a whole century earlier?

"At least they were friends for a while," I said out loud, trying to remind myself of that.

"Elize and Joseph, do you mean?" asked the curator. "Funny you should say that – I've always thought that too, looking at this painting. They've got the same mischief in their eyes, don't they?"

I wondered if I'd tell her about the carvings in the window sill, and then decided to keep it as my own secret for a little while. Maybe over the summer, I'd borrow Dad's camera and take a picture of it, and take it here to the museum so they could put it in a display cabinet for all the world (or at least all of Portbore) to see. . .

"Hey, Stella, can we go now? *Please?*"

I turned round and saw Frankie slouching miserably in the doorway, blowing a giant pink bubble from her mouth.

"Yeah, let's go," I nodded at her, knowing I'd better get her out of here before the bubble burst and she ended up getting gum stuck all over some priceless antique smuggler's swag bag or whatever.

Then the nice lady curator really *would* chuck us out. . .

Chapter 20

Up, up and away-hey-HEY!

"Uh-*ohhhhhhhHHHH*!"

"On a scale of one to ten, Stell," I heard Frankie gasp, "how scared *are* you?"

The coloured lights of the fairground were falling away *frighteningly* fast.

"TEN!" I squealed, holding on so tight to the safety rail folded over our laps that my knuckles were practically *bulging* out of my skin. "What about yooooo-*ooohhhhhHHH*!"

"Nine!" she squeaked back, gripping her hands around the rail every bit as tightly.

Just nine? Well, Frankie always *was* braver than me. And I was kind of relieved to know that she was as freaked out as *I* was about this Big Wheel ride. I took back everything I said about it being a breeze after the London Eye. I mean, yes, the London Eye is high tech and huge, but you're in an enclosed glass pod practically as big as a bus, moving so slowly that you have to keep checking

192

your view of the scenery outside to make sure you've actually *moved*. But this thing; it really hadn't looked that bad when we were standing underneath it a couple of minutes ago. Now that we were up here, though, my insides were swirling around in plain, old-fashioned, non-high-tech *fear*.

THUNK!

"Omigod! What was *that*?" Frankie gasped, as the wheel juddered to a halt, leaving our gondola gently rocking in the evening sea breeze.

"It's OK – look, they're just stopping to let more people on to the next lot of gondolas!" I told Frankie, proud of myself for daring to peek down over the rail – and my dangling legs – to figure out what was going on.

"Don't do that! You're making it swing more!" Frankie begged, sounding suspiciously like a "ten out of ten" on the fear scale to me.

"Look, it's OK – we're moving again!"

"Whose idea was it to come on this thing anyway?" asked Frankie, her voice high and shrieky like she'd just had a suck on a helium balloon.

"Yours!" I laughed at her, forgetting to be worried for a second.

THUNK!

"I wish they wouldn't do that. . ." Frankie moaned. "Y'know, we should have stayed on the dodgems – those lads in the red car were quite cute!"

"Huh?" I choked in surprise. "But you just spent the whole time staring daggers at them and psyching them out!"

"Well, I was only doing it for *your* sake." Frankie shrugged. "Just want everyone in Portbore to know not to bother you."

Hmm . . . I appreciated Frankie acting all protective, but I didn't really *love* the idea of her permanently scaring people away from me, not if I had to *live* here (like it or not).

THUNK!

"Oof!" we both groaned as we came to a standstill again.

"Hey – I don't know what I've hated more today," Frankie began again brightly, once we'd started moving. "Getting my best clothes covered in red dust and cat hairs, hanging about that *borrrrring* museum, or risking my life on this giant bike wheel!"

Things Frankie could usually make me feel: proud, happy, excited, embarrassed (sometimes). But I'd added two new feelings to the list this week: confused (when she blew hot and cold by phone and e-mail) and irritated (that was such a new feeling it had only happened right *now*). Why did she have to have such a downer on Peaches and Portbore?

SCROINGGGGG!

"This is getting ridiculous!" Frankie grumbled, as we thudded to a metal-screeching halt. "How many more people have to get on before they run this ride properly and we can get off?!"

"Frankie," I said warily, "I don't think this is a proper stop. It didn't make the right noise then. . ."

"It didn't?"

"No. It was more of a '*scroing*' than a '*thunk*'."

Normally, saying something daft like that would have given us both the giggles. But when you're dangling worryingly high in thin air, it doesn't exactly feel too normal.

Still, I dared to bend forward again, taking it slowly, slowly this time, to avoid any rocking. We were at the very top of the wheel now, bang on 12 o'clock. And oops . . . the ground seemed freakily far away.

"What's going on?" asked Frankie, leaning as far back as possible on the padded vinyl seat.

"There're some fairground blokes down there, and they're looking a bit worried and sort of . . .

shouting at each other."

"Oh, God. . ." groaned Frankie. "I can't look. I'm going to shut my eyes till they get this thing moving again!"

I wasn't exactly ecstatic about being stranded up here either, but I didn't feel like closing my eyes. The view was just too . . . *wow*.

Directly below, the muddle of music and spangles of coloured lights was kind of mesmerizing. I leant on the rail, ignoring the stressed-out fairground guys, and instead watched as the Saturday night crowds weaved and wound around all the brightly lit attractions. For a second I thought I might have seen a pink meringue hat bobbing amongst all the hairdos and baseball caps, and turned to point it out to Frankie, but she had her eyes shut so tight that I didn't think she'd thank me for forcing her to stare over the edge at the headgear of some mad old lady.

When I turned back, I couldn't see Mrs Sticky Toffee or her meringue hat any more, and didn't know if I had in the first place. There was such a jumble of colour and movement going on down there that a giraffe could wander by in search of the Ghost Train and you wouldn't be sure you'd really seen it.

"What's happening now?" Frankie hissed through clenched teeth.

"Nothing much," I replied, straightening up and gazing around.

More twinkling lights surrounded us in the dark night – none quite as dazzling as the hundreds of coloured bulbs blinking below, but all just as beautiful. To the right, the town spread out, dots of yellowy-white light spilling from every house and streetlamp. To the left, the inky blackness of the sea was broken up with distant sparkles from faraway ships. Over on the headland, even the caravan park looked *almost* picturesque, when all you could see of it was a soft glow peeping out of a myriad of windows. And then above us, there were stars. . .

I tell you something, if I'd been an alien hovering over Portbay tonight, I'd probably think it was the most magical place on –

Bleep!

Much as I was loving the view, I guess the noise I most wanted to hear was the mechanical grind of the Big Wheel starting up again. But failing that, the *bleep!* of an incoming text message was pretty cool too.

"Don't! You're making it wobble again!" Frankie

begged once more, as I let go of the rail and fished my mobile out of my pocket.

"Oops, sorry! Hey, brilliant – it's from Neisha!" I grinned, happy to see our mate's message pop up on the illuminated panel. "She says. . . *Hi – is F there?*"

"I'm here all right," grumbled Frankie, through fear-gritted teeth.

"Look, don't worry," I tried to reassure her, simultaneously texting, *Yeah, F's here – having a mad time!* back to Neisha. "The fairground guys'll get us down soon!"

"They'd *better*," Frankie grumbled unhappily, "or they might end up with hotdog on their heads. . ."

"Huh? You haven't *got* a hotdog to chuck at them!"

"Yeah, but I might hurl the one I ate earlier if they don't hurry up. . ." she groaned miserably.

I was just about to ask her how she could be travel sick when we weren't even *moving* when a familiar bleep interrupted me.

"*Great! So u r not 2 freaked @ Seb news?*" I read aloud, my eyebrows slowly meeting in confusion. "*What* Seb news? Is Neish on about the girl at the Heath?"

I was just about to text back when the phone suddenly disappeared out of my hands.

"*Frankie!*" I gasped. "What did you do *that* for?"

"'Cause I know what Neish is on about, OK?"

"Er, OK," I frowned at her. "So . . . are you going to tell me what it is, then?"

"I'm. . . *I'm* going out with Seb, all right?!" she blurted out, looking half-tearful and half-defensive. "Neish must have thought I'd told you already!"

"*You* and *Seb*?!"

Urgh – tonight was getting more surreal by the millisecond. . .

"Yeah! Me and Seb!"

I felt as wobbly light-headed as I had when we came off the Waltzers earlier.

"But . . . but *you* said it was just some girl hanging out at Hampstead Heath!" I blustered, trying to make sense of something that made no sense at all.

"*I* was the girl hanging out at the Heath!"

"But . . . how? I mean. . . I mean. . . Well, *how*?"

Maybe I wasn't sounding too fluent in English, but Frankie managed to decipher what I was trying to babble.

"Look, I didn't plan for it to happen, Stella! I knew you always liked Seb – *obviously*. It's just that *I* liked him too, but I never ever said 'cause you got in there first. And I didn't know *he* liked me that way too, not till I ran after him when he left your party, when I was trying to get him to sign the photo as a surprise for you."

My limited powers of speech had dried up with the shock. Frankie felt the silence and filled it with more explanation.

"But Seb said he didn't want to write anything on the photo, 'cause he'd come to the party for *me*. He came 'cause he fancied *me*. And I just thought of you and felt terrible and couldn't say anything back. And then he sort of asked me to come up to the Heath the next night and hang out and . . . and . . . I *did*, and he's *lovely* and I like him so, *so* much, Stella, and I'm so, *so* sorry!"

My mouth might not have been working, but my mind certainly was. So *that's* why Seb always made a point of talking to our gang – he was really just talking to Frankie. And the two of them getting together; *that* must have been why Frankie had been off-and-on weird with me this past week.

"All this time you liked Seb too?" I mumbled.

"You should have told me! We tell each other everything!"

I couldn't figure out which was freakier – Frankie going out with Seb behind my back, or Frankie keeping something from me. We were supposed to be mates for ever, no secrets allowed, right?

"I was just looking out for you, like I always do!"

"Huh?" I blinked at her. "How is that looking out for me?"

Hurt, or maybe anger, flitted across Frankie's face.

"Stell, I've *always* taken care of you. I never let anyone hurt your feelings – not even me. So *that's* why I never blabbed about fancying Seb too!"

I crinkled up my nose, not really pleased at hearing her make out like I was some kind of injured bunny who needed constant protection. My silence – and nose crinkling – just seemed to make her *more* hurt and angry.

"You think it's always easy for me, don't you, Stell? Same as Lauren and Neisha and everyone. People look at us and think, Stella, she's the shy one, and there's Frankie, all loud and mouthy. *She's* all right. No one asks me if *I'm* feeling OK or sad or lonely, ever. It's like you leaving London, everyone's, 'Poor Stella – what's it going to be like for her?' But how come it's never, 'Poor Frankie – how's it going to be for her, with her best friend moving away?'"

Now it was *my* turn to feel kind of angry and hurt, and maybe a bit guilty too. I mean, yeah, for the last few months, I'd been all wrapped up in coming here to Portbay, and I guess I hadn't thought about just how bad it would hit Frankie, but now it sounded like she resented me for not noticing how she'd been feeling. But what was I supposed to be – a mind reader? Was it *my* fault if she kept it all to herself?

And never mind that – there was still the fact that she went out with Seb about five seconds after I left town, and there were still a couple of questions about that that I needed answers to. . .

"Seb came over to me at the party and told me that he'd always thought I was kind of cute!" I blurted out.

"But you *are* cute, Stella!" said Frankie, rolling her eyes. "He was just being nice and giving you a compliment 'cause it was your leaving party!"

Talk about feeling gutted. . .

"But what about the Polaroid?" I frowned at Frankie. "He wrote that message on the Polaroid!"

Frankie bit her lip and stared at me . . . and the truth flooded into my befuddled brain.

"*You* wrote that, didn't you?"

"Well, I didn't want to disappoint you! I did a pretty good job of disguising my writing, didn't I?"

My so-called best friend suddenly seemed to realize that she had no hope of an answer to that question and wordlessly handed me my phone back.

And that's how we stayed for endless minutes, silently stuck in mid-air, with no way to escape each other, though that was the exact thing I was sure we both wanted to do. . .

"*CAWWWW!!*"

"Stella!" Frankie screeched, as loudly as the seagull that had swooped in front of us, bobbing on lazy currents of air and amusing itself with our predicament.

"It's all right – it's just a gull!" I snapped at her. "It won't hurt –"

Before I could explain that there was no danger of the bird dive-bombing us, the dopey thing only floated over and landed with a gentle thud on the back of our gondola.

"Eeek!" squeaked Frankie, yanking the hood of

her top up and pulling the drawstrings so tight that only her panic-stricken eyes peeked out.

The bird blinked blankly at her, wondering what all the fuss was about.

"What does it want?" a shaky, muffled voice came out of the hood.

"A fairy cake, I think."

"A *what*?"

And then I had a vision – if an alien *did* happen to be hovering in the vicinity right now, what would it see? One freckle-nosed, grumpy girl (me), Kenny from *South Park* (Frankie) and a large dorky bird (the fairy-cake fan), swaying gently in mid-air on a jammed fairground ride. It was too ridiculous for words. Actually, it was too ridiculous to keep a straight *face*. . .

"What are you laughing at?" Frankie muffled from inside her hood, probably alarmed that I'd turned psycho and was about to chuck her out of the gondola or something. But I was giggling too much to explain to her, and a few worried seconds later, I saw her eyes crinkle up with giggles too.

And you know a couple of somethings that occurred to me then? The first something was that already, although I'd only been here in Portbay a week, London – and Seb – seemed as far away as the stars spangling above me. It was just that Frankie's confession didn't *bother* me as much as I thought it would. Well, not the one about Seb, anyway. The stuff about how she wasn't as tough as she made out bothered me quite a *bit*, which brought me on to the *other* something: Elize and Joseph had lost touch; Nana Jones and Grandad Eddie had lost touch. Losing touch with people that mattered was awful, and no *way* was I going to let that happen to me and Frankie. No stupid boy with some stupid lopsided grin in stupid London was going to come between me and my oldest, bestest mate. . .

"Frankie?" I said, when the giggles eased off.

"Uh-huh?" she mumbled, tugging the cord on her hood loose.

"From now on, no more secrets. We tell each other everything. *Everything*. OK?"

"OK!"

The seagull flapped away when me and Frankie started hugging, probably off to see if it could find any leftover toffee apples or Portbay rock or whatever weird food was its second favourite after fairy cakes. . .

Chapter 21

Fluffy burgers and undercover freckles

Ah . . . it was a perfect party, on a perfect summer Sunday afternoon. Smoke was billowing from the barbecue, neighbours were chatting, small children were headbutting each other and the sun was glinting off the skip. . .

"So what do you think of the house, Auntie V?" I asked, as my aunt glided over towards me and Frankie with a paper plate in one hand and a look of pure horror on her face.

"Well, Stella, my little star, it's nice . . . if you like cowsheds," she shrugged, placing the plate on the nearest window sill with a clang of silver and amber bracelets. I noticed she'd only taken one, neat bite out of her burger.

"Listen, girls, I'm only going to tell you this once," Auntie V suddenly lowered her voice to a whisper. "Stick to the hotdogs – the burgers are like burnt dog food!"

Frankie and me swapped glances and tried not

to giggle. Not just 'cause it was funny the way Auntie V was slagging off Dad's barbecuing skills (specially when she was smiling and waving to him at the same time), but because we knew *another* reason not to touch the dog-food burgers. This morning, we'd been too busy e-mailing Neisha and the others (telling them everything was out in the open and everything was cool) that we hadn't gone with Dad to pick up Auntie V from the station. Once we'd pressed the last "send" on the last message, me and Frankie ambled through to the kitchen – and caught my harassed mum washing fluff off the frozen burgers under the kitchen tap.

"The boys got hold of them," Mum had explained, red-faced, to us. "They were rolling them along the floor having a race!"

"Who won?" Frankie had joked, till she'd spotted Jake and Jamie pouring half a mug of cold tea into one of her trainers. . .

"We'll stick to the hotdogs, then!" I smiled at Auntie V, pretending to take her advice.

I wish I'd given her a bit of advice too – don't wear white trousers near small boys. I don't think she'd spotted the greasy handprints around her knee, where Jake had hugged her as soon as she'd arrived.

"You know I love them dearly, Stella," Auntie V began chatting again. "But your parents are insane. Who has a house-warming party in their driveway, with a skip full of rubble in full view?"

"Yeah, but they couldn't have it in the back garden," I started to defend Mum and Dad. "They haven't cleared it yet and I think they're scared there're bear traps in there!"

"Good to see you've still got a got a sense of humour, Stella," she turned and smiled, scrutinizing my face. "I was worried I'd find you in floods of tears today, stuck here in Cowshed Town, so far away from Frankie etc.!"

"It won't feel like they're too far away, not when we can e-mail and stuff," I told her.

"And Stella can come to London to visit us!" Frankie chipped in.

"Or you and Neish and Lauren and everyone can come down *here*!" I pointed out to Frankie.

"What, so we can play crummy crazy golf or something dullsville like that?" Frankie grinned at me.

I think it was going to take her a few visits to get used to Portbay, like I had. Mad as it sounded, I wasn't in too much of a hurry to rush back to Kentish Town – not when I had gallons more to find out about this weird place that was now home.

"You know something?" Auntie V suddenly said, narrowing her eyes and putting a hand out to stroke my curls. "All this sea air seems to suit you, Stella. You're sounding – I mean, *looking* really good."

"Now, you've got to watch the truth; it has a funny habit of slipping out, even when you hold it back!": that's another of Aunt Esme's favourite sayings. And my *real*-life aunt might have just corrected herself, but I knew what she meant, and I knew Auntie V was right. I *was* sounding better. I'd always been able to chat away easily to my parents and Frankie, but since I'd been here, I wasn't just saving my words for *their* ears. And the words I was saying didn't start with a stammer . . . well, not as often as they used to.

And I liked that. A *lot*. I liked the fact that I could be a whole new Stella in this town. I wasn't Stella the non-star, and I wasn't Frankie's silent, shy friend. To anyone who might be interested, I was the new girl from London, with too many freckles but really great hair. . .

"Hey, I think your dad's waving you over!" Frankie suddenly nudged me, pointing to Dad's blond head sticking up above a sea of bobbing, chatting neighbourly faces.

I started over towards him, Frankie following. In our wake, at the cracking sound of another headbutt, Auntie V lunged across the driveway shouting, "Animal! Gonzo! Would you two *stop* doing that!"

"Stella!" Dad beamed, waving a barbecue fork around with a blackened sausage stuck on the prongs. "This is Maggie, the lady I was telling you about, from next door!"

Oh, yeah, the ex-teacher. She was slim, grey-haired and sporty-looking. Er . . . I *really* hoped that friendly smile aimed in my direction didn't mean she was about to offer me extra tuition *after* all.

"Hello, Stella! Your father said you were keen to find out about the artist who lived in your cottage. And I thought this might just solve the mystery!"

Gingerly, with a quick glance at Frankie, I took the old yellowed newspaper she was holding out.

"I found it in my loft yesterday, when I was storing a few things. It was used to line an old chest of drawers. . ."

Frankie leant her chin on my shoulder as I opened up the crackly, fragile paper. The date at the top of the front page read, 12 July, 1930. I didn't know what I was looking for at first, but with a nudge from Maggie, I turned to the second page of the *Portbay Chronicle* and saw a grainy black-and-white photo of a very, *very* old lady, sitting in a pretty garden with an easel in front of her, a floppy felt hat shading her eyes from the summer sun. On the easel was a familiar half-finished painting of a fairy, and on a small table by her side was a pretty china cup and a wooden box for her pencils. Because of the angle, you couldn't see the letters *E G* carved on the top of the box, but I *knew* Elize Grainger's initials would be there.

"'*A Hundred Years of History! Miss Grainger celebrates her centenary with her favourite hobby, painting*'," Frankie read aloud. "'*It may be a far cry from her former palatial home in Sugar Bay, but for the last thirty years, Miss Elize Grainger has been very happy in the much smaller but nonetheless most commodious surroundings of Foxglove Cottage.*' God, they were pretty fond of using big words in those days, weren't they? I mean, what's 'commodious' supposed to mean?"

Frankie was still asking her question when I mumbled my thanks to Maggie and ran off around the side of the house in the direction of the garden. . .

*

"That smelly cat isn't in here, is it?"

"No," I told Frankie as she followed me into the outhouse. "And he's *not* smelly. Well, he *is*, but in a good way. . ."

Frankie didn't look convinced – just like Portbay, it was going to take a bit of time for her to fall for Peaches' scuzzy charms.

After walking in warily, Frankie pulled up the armchair that Peaches liked to sleep in and sat down beside me at the table. (I didn't dare think about the fact that she was wearing her new black trousers. . .)

"So what's that you're looking at?" she asked, pointing at the chipped china cup and wooden box I'd taken down from the shelves.

"*This*, actually," I told her, holding up the blackened brass button that had been in the box when I first came across it. "I think it belonged to—"

"Joseph! The servant guy, right? He was wearing some fancy jacket with buttons like that in the painting, wasn't he?"

So Frankie had been paying more attention than

212

I thought at the museum yesterday! Or maybe it was just that she'd tried *really* hard to listen this morning, when I'd taken her out to the den and explained why the house at Sugar Bay had fascinated me so much. And I knew Frankie really did understand now, specially when she got all choked up as I finished carving *Stella + Frankie, m8s 4eva, 2004* on the rickety window sill of the outhouse.

"She must have kept this as a memento of her old friend!" I said softly, turning the button over in my fingers.

"I guess. . ." nodded Frankie, her braids swaying across her shoulders. "Hey, you'll have to get this newspaper story framed, and the photo your mum dug out last night!"

Oh, yes, today I'd found out a chunk of the history of the house, but last night – after we'd finally been set free from the Big Wheel – me and Frankie arrived home to discover that Mum had unearthed a chunk of history about *me*.

"Stella, I swear I never knew they were there," Mum had told me, as she stared at the photo she'd handed to me. "Ever since I was little, I remember my mum wearing heavy make-up. I always thought it was just her style; I didn't know she was slapping it on to cover her freckles!"

The black-and-white photo of Nana Jones in all her 17-year-old freckly glory was now pinned to my corkboard, till Woolworths opened tomorrow morning and I could get a decent frame for it.

"He was pretty cute-looking, your grandad, wasn't he?" Frankie commented, leaning forward and squinting at the handsome young guy hugging my Nana Jones so proudly, laughter dimples visible in his dark skin.

"Yep," I nodded, just as happy and delighted as I had been last night that Mum had finally found one of those elusive "spare moments" and come across this photo that she'd never known existed in Nana Jones's stuff. And it was great that it had nudged her memory a little.

"Of course! I *do* remember my mother saying he worked on a fairground. That's why he was only there for the summer, then moved on!"

"Weird coincidence him working on a fair when we've just been to one!" Frankie murmured, her eyes skimming over the gaudily painted Waltzers in the background, covered in ornate decorations of fat cherubs and flighty fairies.

"Isn't it?" I agreed, though I didn't think that for a *second*. Secretly, I didn't believe in coincidences any more, not since I'd come to Portbay. . .

"Prrrp!"

Uh-oh – Frankie had better prepare herself for Peaches and his Amazing Shedding Hair. Any second now he'd come bounding through my still-to-be-repaired broken windowpane (minus the lethal shards, which Dad had removed, only causing himself one deep cut and a few scratches).

And then I heard another familiar voice, and peered outside.

"Er, hello there, pussy!" Auntie V was saying, veering away as Peaches tried to curl himself and his ginger fur around her legs. "Have you seen Stella etc., hmm? I've got to tell them it's safe to come back now – the new neighbours have eaten all the dog burgers!"

I grinned, partly at Auntie V's joke and partly because I *really* liked the sound of what she'd just said: Stella etc.

OK, so at the moment, Stella etc. consisted of me (Stella), and an ugly, fat, funny-smelling cat called Peaches. But give me time (like a whole summer holiday), and who knew who'd be part of the "etc."?

I couldn't *wait* to find out.

"Oh, there you are!" said Auntie V, sticking

her head around the outhouse door and frowning through her smile, as if she was terrified that a family of spiders might drop into her serum'd hair. "Jake and Jamie just fed the cheesecake your mum made to the collie from across the road, so your neighbour Maggie's brought around a tray of biscuits that she just made. Coming to get one?"

"What kind are they?" asked Frankie dubiously. "I hate biscuits – they're so boring."

"Well, they're not *biscuits* exactly," Auntie V shrugged, oblivious to the cobweb that had attached itself to the side of her head. "They're old-fashioned, and in those funny paper cups. What are they called again? Fairy cakes! Yes, *that's* it!"

"My favourite!" I grinned, following my aunt out into the sunlight.

Walking around to the front of the cottage, I heard Frankie curse as Peaches lovingly wound his way between her legs, shedding hairs and practically tripping her up with every step.

And me? Well, I was busy scouring the sky for signs of seagulls with a sweet tooth. . .

From:		Frankie
To:		*stella*
Subject:		Re: Helloooooooooooo!

Hi Stella!

No worries about missing my phone call – if you had to help look after the Muppets, then you had to help look after the Muppets. (By the way, tell your mum that the bite-mark on my arm has practically healed. And tell Jamie I'm going to bite him back when he's big enough!)

But seriously, thanks for sending me that stuff Stell – that first week you left was weird for us both in different ways, wasn't it, and it's great to hear it all from your side. I'd love to sit down and write things from my side now too, but I won't because I'm way, way too lazy. Ha!

Nothing much happening this end. Well, OK, things are going brilliantly with Seb, but I'm not going to go on about that 'cause I still feel a bit weird about the whole thing with you and me and him. I know it bugs you when I say that, but tough. Double ha!

Miss you ☹, but m8s 4eva ☺!
Frankie

PS Tell Peaches that I still keep finding his hair everywhere!

PPS Send more attachments – I need to know PROPERLY what's going on. Like who was that boy who answered your mobile the other day, hmm? You'd better tell me more SOON, Stella!!